WAITING FOR A FOREVER LOVE

LOST LOVE
BOOK TWO

WILLA BLAIR

OUVERHEBERBOOKS

All rights reserved.

No part of this publication may be sold, copied, distributed, reproduced or transmitted in any form or by any means, mechanical or digital, including photocopying and recording or by any information storage and retrieval system without the prior written permission of both the publisher, Oliver Heber Books and the author, Willa Blair, except in the case of brief quotations embodied in critical articles and reviews.

PUBLISHER'S NOTE: This is a work of fiction. Names, characters, places, and incidents either are the product of the author's imagination or are used fictitiously. Any resemblance to actual persons, living or dead, business establishments, events, or locales is entirely coincidental.

Waiting for a Forever Love Copyright © by Linda Williams

Cover art by Dar Albert at Wicked Smart Designs

Published by Oliver-Heber Books

This title was previously published

0 9 8 7 6 5 4 3 2 1

PRAISE FOR WILLA BLAIR AND...

WAITING FOR THE LAIRD: "Ian Patterson is hero to dream for..."

— NIGHT OWL REVIEWS TOP PICK

HEART OF STONE: "...Fast paced and well written with passion, charismatic characters and romantic, thrilling storyline. Perfectly wicked and dangerous! Simply put, WOW!"

— MY BOOK ADDICTION AND MORE

HIGHLAND HEALER: "Stealing a woman's heart has never been so dangerous."

— THE ROMANCE REVIEWS

THE HEALER'S GIFT: "A story of mystery, regret, hope, danger, and trust...The characters are endearing, the story is fulfilling, and the set up for the remainder of the series presents an open invitation to dive right in. THE HEALER'S GIFT is a highly recommended read."

— FRESH FICTION

HIGHLAND SEER: "…this is different enough from other Highland romances to stand out from the pack. Ms. Blair's writing style is natural and evocative…"

— ROMANTIC HISTORICAL REVIEWS

HIGHLAND TROTH: "…trickling danger and suspense in perfect amounts…Scottish romance at its best!"

— IND'TALE MAGAZINE

WHEN HIGHLAND LIGHTNING STRIKES: "Ms. Blair is a consummate storyteller…Can't wait for more from this magical author."

— MY BOOK ADDICTION AND MORE

HIS HIGHLAND ROSE: "Another awesome Scottish Romance!"

— MY BOOK ADDICTION AND MORE

HIS HIGHLAND HEART: "The plot was honestly a masterpiece. It was well thought out and orchestrated. Right out the gate I was hooked! The hero had immediate book boyfriend appeal."

— LONG AND SHORT REVIEWS

HIS HIGHLAND LOVE: "Fiery passion burns bright in HIS HIGHLAND LOVE! Readers who enjoy Highland romance should definitely try Willa Blair's books."

— BOOKS & BENCHES

HIS HIGHLAND BRIDE: "Ms. Blair has delivered a wonderful and captivating read in this book where the chemistry between this couple was strong; the romance hot…"

— BOOK MAGIC, UNDER A SPELL WITH EVERY PAGE

And for Author Willa Blair: "I thoroughly enjoy Blair's work and recommend her Scottish love stories to all!"

— ELIZA KNIGHT, USA TODAY BESTSELLING AUTHOR

AUTHOR'S NOTE

Waiting for a Forever Love was previously published as *When You Find Love*, a finalist in the Short Contemporary category of the 2021 BookSellers' Best Award. If you read the earlier book, I hope you will enjoy Caitlin Paterson's and Holt Ridley's new, expanded romance. It has been rebranded, new scenes and details have been added, and the emotional story deepened. And as you can see, it has a gorgeous new cover.

Oh, and for his fans, Fergus, from *Waiting for the Laird*, the first book in this series, still makes an appearance at the end.

If the story is new to you, I hope you have a wonderful time. Read on!

CHAPTER 1

LONG ISLAND, NY, EARLY DECEMBER, PRESENT DAY

After the long flight from Scotland, Caitlin Paterson couldn't use either of her favorite sources of caffeine to help her combat jet lag. She'd been hired to research and catalog the contents of a private estate *seaside cottage* in the Hamptons recently inherited by a Holt Ridley from California. With so much at stake, she had to make a good first impression, which ruled out coffee or tea spills on her clothes.

She hoped her contact at the National Museum who'd recommended her for the job was right about its scope and potential value to her career. Added to Caitlin's recent work assessing a hidden cache of Jacobite treasures, this trip across the pond could cement her professional reputation. And that should guarantee her selection for her dream position in Inverness at the Highland Museum, which would make the uncomfortable trip worthwhile.

She shifted on the taxi's sprung seat, trying for the hundredth time to find a position even slightly more comfortable than the one in the airplane's economy cabin that she'd recently vacated. Giving up, she let herself dream of a leisurely sail across the Atlantic, complete with one's own stateroom, gourmet meals, interesting dinner companions and, when one desired, glorious solitude.

And icebergs, rough seas, and motion sickness for a week, she consoled herself.

Still, she couldn't complain. The advance from the Ridley estate's solicitor, rather *lawyer* as they were called here, would have allowed her to fly business class. She hadn't because she hated to waste so much money on the elevated fare. Stifling a yawn, she vowed it was a mistake she wouldn't repeat.

A sudden slowdown and turn pulled Caitlin back to her present circumstance. The driver spoke into a box outside a large gate, which opened smoothly once he said her name. They had arrived.

As the taxi pulled up the long tree-lined approach, Caitlin's stomach sank. The lawyer's description had not done this place justice. She had done her research, she had. But the family was either social-media ignorant or exceedingly private. Or both. Nothing she'd learned about the resident family or this estate in the little she could find online prepared her for its sheer size. She'd never heard a pile like the one before her now called a cottage. It might be as big as her cousin Ian and his wife Lara's estate, Cairn

Dubh, in the Highlands of Scotland. Depending on what she found inside, she could be here for months rather than the two weeks she'd anticipated.

The taxi stopped at the front portico, a massive, white semicircle that fronted the stone and stucco edifice. "That'll be two hundred and eighty-five dollars, miss," the driver told her as he opened his door.

He got out, opened the trunk, and began unloading her bags while Caitlin dug through her purse for a credit card, mentally subtracting the fare from the advance she'd been given to make the trip. The fare seemed quite high, even discounting the conversion rate from Scottish pounds to dollars. And she couldn't forget the tip. Americans expected a tip, right?

The front door to the estate opened, and a dapper older gentleman dressed in a dark suit and bow tie approached. He had a word with the driver, picked up Caitlin's bags, and turned.

"Sir, where are ye going with those?"

The driver opened her door and stepped back. "He took care of everything. Just follow him inside."

"Aye? Very good." Caitlin stuffed her wallet back in her purse, and after looking around to make sure she wasn't going to leave something behind, she got out. "Thank you," she mumbled and headed up the steps, barely aware when the taxi pulled away.

The gentleman waited for her at the front door, a confection in beveled glass set in wood painted white to match the portico's trim. "Welcome to Hampton Dales," he announced without offering his hand. "I am Mr. Farrell, in charge of this property for the Ridley family. You may dispense with the title and call me Farrell." He opened the front door, gestured her inside, and again, picked up her bags. "If you'll allow me, I will show you to your rooms, and later, give you a tour of the house."

He sounded like a bloody English butler minus the accent. She heard some New York in his speech, calling on her recollection of American cop shows she'd seen. He didn't sound like Ian's wife, Lara, so he was not from California like the heir to this great pile. Caitlin managed a polite nod before she responded. "Thank you, Farrell, I'd appreciate that."

She entered the house but had to pause in the high-ceilinged foyer to admire a sparkling chandelier. "Waterford?"

"Baccarat, miss. I apologize for the lack of seasonal decorations, but given the circumstance this year…"

"Of course. Such a celebration would seem out of place."

"Thank you for understanding. Now, you must be tired from your trip. Follow me."

Farrell led her to a suite of rooms larger than her flat at home, including a sitting room, a bedroom and a privy that reminded her of the huge Roman baths in the English city of Bath, complete with luxurious towels, scented soaps and a plush robe. If it included a stocked kitchen and a telly so she could watch her favorite TV shows, she would never have to leave it.

"I trust this will be suitable, miss."

"Of course," Caitlin replied, still intent on studying every aspect of her new surroundings.

The sitting room included a wood-burning fireplace, now cheerfully warming and illuminating two facing wing-back chairs upholstered in what looked to be butter-soft suede the color of cream. They were anchored by a navy-blue leather sofa, broad and deep enough for her and at least two other people to relax comfortably.

An ornately carved four-poster large enough to accommodate a caber toss, with a mountain of pillows at its head, dominated the bedroom. Farrell then showed her a walk-in closet that included a built-in chest of drawers, a wealth of shelves, and its own time zone.

"I believe this will do nicely," Caitlin managed to say. "I didn't bring enough with me to use a fraction of this space."

"The estate has provided an allowance, should you require any new clothing, coats or shoes. You may not be prepared for the change of seasons here on the water."

"I come from Scotland. Yer weather canna be any worse than a Scottish winter."

Farrell cleared his throat, apparently too polite to disagree directly.

"As you wish, miss. Dinner will be served in the small dining room at seven o'clock. If you would like something before then, you have only to ask."

Caitlin's stomach picked that moment to rumble. "I believe I would— just something light to hold me over for a couple of hours. It is five?"

"Five o'clock, yes. I'll have Mrs. Smith bring a tray

straight up. Wine, cheese, fruit, paté, and crackers? Or would you prefer something hot? Soup, perhaps?"

"The cheese tray sounds lovely. Thank you. Will Mr. Ridley be joining me for dinner?"

"I'm sorry, but no. He is, at this moment, still in California. He's expected in a few days. By then, perhaps you will have a completed a preliminary survey and developed a sense of the furnishings contained in the house. An estimate of the time you will need to complete your assessment and catalog will, no doubt, be useful."

Caitlin suspected that was more than a suggestion. Rather, he'd just given her fair warning. The boss would want information when he arrived. "Perhaps after dinner, you will give me the tour you mentioned."

"I'd be honored." He didn't quite bow but inclined his head. "I'll leave you to relax." He glanced toward the door to the Roman spa attached to her suite. "Mrs. Smith will be up with a tray in a few minutes and will leave it on the writing-table, there."

He indicated the surface with a nod in its direction, just in case she decided to take advantage of the sybaritic pleasures of that bath. He didn't have to say it. The implication was clear. And, with a glance over her shoulder, Caitlin agreed. It was a damn good idea.

Farrell excused himself and left her to unpack and settle in. Her tray arrived ten minutes later, just as Caitlin had begun to hang the clothes she'd brought in the cavernous closet. She missed meeting the Mrs. Smith delivering it. By the time she noticed a slight noise in the outer room and went to investigate, the woman was gone.

Caitlin finished stowing her things and nibbled on the contents of the tray, then headed for the Roman bath. She might as well enjoy herself if she was going to be working and eating alone until her employer showed up demanding a progress report.

∼

SILICON VALLEY

Holt Ridley frowned at his executive assistant as she placed a stack of correspondence on the exact center of his desk, a certified letter displayed prominently on top.

"Another one?" He stood and flipped quickly through the rest of the stack while he told her. "Send it back, marked *Refused*. Do the same with any others that arrive from this law firm." He proffered the letter.

When she didn't take it from him, he looked up, surprised.

She shook her head. "Sir, I'm afraid that won't stop the inquiries."

Holt shrugged. "They can send all they like. I'm not interested in what they're offering." He tossed the registered letter into the trash receptacle next to his desk.

"That's not going to work, either…"

Holt sighed. The doggedness that made her an excellent executive assistant did have its drawbacks. She wouldn't stop until she said what was on her mind.

"Why not?"

"A Mr. Thornton is waiting for you in the outer office."

"Thornton as in—"

"Barclay, Thornton, and Barclay, yes." She held out a heavily embossed business card.

Holt took it and gave it a glance, then added it to the trash, along with the registered letter from the man's firm. "Send him away."

"I tried, but he won't budge. He threatened to *camp out in the reception area*," she said and added air quotes, "if that's what it takes to get a few moments of your time."

Holt glared at the coffered ceiling above him in frustration. "That bad, huh?"

"He won't leave until he sees you."

She was very good at reading people— another reason she'd been with him for years— so if she thought Mr. Thornton was prepared to wait him out, Holt could be certain the man would not relent. Too bad she hadn't told him what she thought about Helen Conroe. He sighed and fought back a curse. "Send him in, then. We can't have a squatter in our outer office."

Not wanting to give this Mr. Thornton the opportunity to sit down and thereby prolong their meeting, Holt stayed on his feet.

The lawyer, when he entered, was not the bulldog in a thousand-dollar suit Holt expected. He was slight and graying, wearing something off-the-rack and entirely too warm for the local climate.

"Mr. Ridley." He glanced aside at the visitor's chair and straightened his thin shoulders. "You're a hard man to reach." Thornton plowed on before Holt had the chance to ask him what the hell he was doing in California after sending interminable official correspondence that Holt ignored. "Since I'm certain your assistant gave you my card, I'll get straight to the point. Your lack of response these past five months has forced me to come to you directly. Your great-aunt's estate cannot sit unclaimed forever."

Holt wondered how Thornton wound up a partner in a Long Island law firm. He was certain he detected a hint of a cultured British accent, but even without it, Thornton's obsequious phrasing gave away his homeland, as did his carefully neutral expression. Holt was having none of it. "As far as I'm concerned, it can. You've made a long trip for nothing."

The man had to be exasperated, but his face remained calm, his demeanor unruffled.

"On the contrary, Mr. Ridley. I've brought your great-aunt's last will and testament, along with papers for you to sign. I hope we can conclude our business amicably, sir, because I also have with me a summons from the district court of Suffolk County, New York that I have been authorized and directed to serve should we fail in our discussion."

Holt frowned. "On what grounds?"

Thornton's expression didn't change. "Abandonment of historic property. The house known as Hampton Dales is on the register of historical places in the county. I understand from your great-aunt that the contents, family heirlooms and such, are even more valuable than the house and property overlooking the Sound." He cleared his throat and continued, "Which are quite valuable themselves. She left it all to you, sir."

"I don't want it." He had made his own money. He didn't need hers. His great-aunt had treated his mother so badly, that even after she escaped the old woman's abuse, his mother remained certain the estate must also be infected with the curse on the family she claimed was passed through her uncle's line. Holt had never taken seriously the idea of a family curse, much less that it could infest a structure they inhabited. But he had enough of his own bad memories about that place to keep him on a therapist's couch for the rest of his life.

"Nonetheless," Thornton said, "the will is binding on you."

Holt heard a trace of irritation creep into Thornton's voice, which suited him. He had heard quite enough, and often enough, from Thornton and his law firm partners to harbor more than a hint of irritation of his own. He'd begun to fear they would never quit but use some nefarious automation to keep sending letter after letter and make phone call after phone call. Irritation in Thornton's tone told Holt there were people behind this and people could be manipulated. "Then I'll sell it." And good riddance.

"You may do that, sir, after ninety day's residency."

"What?" The. Hell? The sudden urge to sit down swamped Holt, weakening his knees. He fought it.

"Your great-aunt stipulates in her will that you occupy the property for three months before selling it, interrupted only by necessary and reasonable— short— periods which

I must approve. She anticipated your antipathy and took measures to ensure you did not reject her bequest without due consideration."

Holt's hands balled into fists. He flexed them open at his sides and forced himself to leave them there. He refused to cross his arms protectively over his chest. He would not betray how his memories unsettled him to this…this— he took a breath. Person. His great-aunt's solicitor, he told himself, was only doing his job. Holt didn't have to like it, but he would not get his way by further antagonizing the man. What had seemed a game, stymying a law firm a moment ago, had taken a sudden and very inconvenient turn.

"That's impossible. My home and my business are here. I cannot spend months on the opposite coast, no matter what my great-aunt's will demands."

Thornton set his battered briefcase on the visitor chair, opened it, then pulled out three folded documents covered in craft paper. "Her last will and testament and transfer document for your signature as heir," he said, ignoring Holt's objections and placing it on his desk. "A copy of tax assessments, surveys, blueprints of the house, and a preliminary inventory of its contents— with no valuation applied to said inventory," he continued as he added a thicker bundle beside the first. "Per your great-aunt's instructions, I have retained an expert in British antiques and antiquities to do a thorough assessment and valuation of the contents. Said expert has arrived and is being cared for by the estate's staff, a Mr. Farrell and Mrs. Smith." The last bundle he retained. "This is the summons with which I hesitate to burden you." He gestured at the documents he'd placed on the desk. "Dealing with those would be simpler."

Like anyone, Holt hated his wishes being ignored, but he held onto his shredding temper. The man had come a long way to give him something valuable, even if it held no value for Holt. "You can take them all with you when you leave," he said as politely as he could manage.

Perversely, Thornton laid the summons on Holts' desk, alongside the other packets. "I regret the necessity," he said quietly, then straightened and spoke up. "Mr. Holt Ridley, you are hereby served and required by Suffolk County to appear in court to determine the disposition of your great-aunt's bequest."

Cold fury shot ice down Holt's spine. He gestured toward the door, a clear invitation to vacate his office. "My lawyers will see about that," he responded in as even a tone as he could manage.

Once Thornton closed his now-empty brief case, nodded and left, Holt dropped into his plush leather swivel chair and leaned back. He glared at the pile of documents on his desk, the summons on top. His great-aunt had caught him neatly in the sticky strands of her web. After the way she'd treated his mother, he couldn't imagine why she was giving him the estate, and it was too late to ask her. Guilt, perhaps? Or was he her only living relative? He'd been too irritated at the intrusion and the reason for Thornton's visit to think to ask. But his lawyers could find out easily enough.

If he didn't sort this out, he was headed for weeks of legal proceedings about his aunt's estate. After dealing with

Helen Conroe and her lawyers for the last six months, the idea made his belly ache. He'd recently learned an expensive lesson when Helen tried to seduce him into a partnership with her. It didn't take long before he realized she wanted Ridley Communications' proprietary algorithms more than him. When he ended their relationship, he never imagined she'd sink to industrial theft, but she wasted no time infiltrating his company. When her man got caught leaving with Ridley company secrets, Holt had the employee arrested and took Helen to court.

Holt knew Helen would keep coming after his company. She'd made it personal. He wasn't ready to sell. He'd turned down friendly offers in the past. Still, a white knight with deep pockets could help him fight off any attempt at a hostile takeover.

He eyed the documents that Thornton left.

Perhaps he'd been too hasty in tossing the lawyer out of his office. Thornton had mentioned cash reserves and investments, available only when Holt took possession of his great-aunt's estate. The amount of those funds had not been specified, but even so, selling the English antiques from the old place seemed a sure-fire way to raise a lot of capital. The house and property were worth millions according to Mr. Thornton and to Holt's mother before she died, but adding the contents could be worth enough to improve his cash flow and attract a trustworthy — and temporary— investor. He hoped they were right about the value of the estate.

The documents were precisely where Thornton had placed them on the visitor side of Holt's desk. He regarded them as one might regard a toxic spill, with reluctance to approach or touch them. Yet, he couldn't let his antipathy for his mother's relative override his good business sense. Those documents led to a resource only he could use, even if it meant spending three months across the country on Long Island. It might be worth it.

Holt hadn't thought to ask, and Thornton hadn't mentioned what happened to the estate in the event Holt answered the summons and outright refused the bequest. Well, it didn't matter. He wasn't going to refuse it. He was going to use it.

He picked up the phone on his desk and told his assistant to book a flight.

~

*H*olt knew better than to take the commercial redeye to JFK. That overnight flight always put him in a bad mood, but his jet was in for maintenance scheduled long before the need for this trip came up. Tired and hungry after finding nothing decent to eat in his arrival terminal, he stared out the window on the short hop out to Islip, wondering how long it would take to hook up with a ride-share driver. Instead, a well-dressed older man in the arrivals lounge held a sign with his name on it.

"I'm Farrell, your great-aunt Amelia's assistant. Luggage, sir?"

Holt glanced at his briefcase. He'd put the lawyer's paperwork there, so he'd hang onto it. He handed over his go-bag, something he took whenever he traveled. One never knew when a flight, even his private plane, would be delayed or canceled by weather or mechanical failure. "I plan to catch a return flight as soon as possible. Let's go." The ride out to Hampton Dales would give him time to get his equilibrium back. He squinted in the morning sunshine as Farrell led him to a black limo and indicated a thermos full of hot coffee.

As he'd hoped, at the end of the hour and a half drive, Holt felt much better. The limo pulled through the gate that broke the line of the high, dense hedges lining the lane and made its way up the long drive to the main house. Farrell opened the back seat door and stood aside.

Holt swung out of the car and then turned to regard the house. Still, an overblown, overlarge tribute to the 19th century, with newer wings added to blend with the style but always looking oddly out of place.

The whole sordid mess was his now, evil spirits and all. If he was truly stuck here for three months, he'd spend the time doing what he could to exorcise the bad feelings he retained, and then sell the damned lot. Let them become someone else's problem.

He started for the steps leading to the double front doors, then paused and turned back to Farrell. "Is the appraiser still here?"

Farrell glanced toward the house. "Yes, sir. She arrived the day before yesterday and went immediately to work."

"She? I assumed the appraiser was a man."

Farrell's upper lip quirked. "Not in the least, Mr. Ridley."

Whatever that meant. At the moment, Holt didn't care.

He wanted this visit finished, his business concluded, and himself on the first available flight west. He shook his head and mounted the stone steps, Farrell on his heels. On the porch, he paused, allowing Farrell to open the door. "Not locked?"

"Not when the staff is in residence— we're well away from the village. The rare visitor tends to be from the waterside." At Holt's frown, he added, "From the occasional boat run aground. The point is wreathed in shifting sands, sir."

"Indeed. I'd forgotten." He'd beached a small rowboat here during a summer squall when he was fourteen but had not dared approach the house. What would he say to the people who'd turned out his mother? *Hello, I'm the grand-nephew you've never welcomed...I need your help?* He could imagine how that appeal would have been greeted— with a slammed door. Instead, he'd rescued himself, walking a mile in driving rain and wind along the beach. Thankfully, he'd reached another estate before the coastline rose too high or steep for him to climb. The staff there had let him call his mother for a ride home. She hadn't been happy to hear where he'd landed and warned him never to go near the estate again. He'd defended himself, determined to retrieve his boat, blaming the storm, and they'd argued. He still regretted some of the things he'd said.

He wondered if the remains of his little boat still littered the sand. Likely not, after years of tides and storms. Too bad he hadn't been able to retrieve it. He had a sudden fit of nostalgia, sadness that struck him unexpectedly now and again. Grimly, he shook it off and entered the grand foyer.

The first thing he noticed was the height of the ceiling. It soared 20 feet, the cavernous space filled with a large, sparkling crystal chandelier. Ostentatious, he thought, especially for a place referred to as a beach cottage. Glossy black and white tiles laid on the diagonal drew the eye down a long hallway to large windows, or perhaps french doors, leading to the back garden, lush mounds of green punctuated by bright pops of colorful flowers. The blues of water and sky peeked through gaps in the landscaping. Doors lined the hallway left and right, open and giving glimpses of the rooms within, except for one set. Walnut, he surmised, the closed doors dark and rich against pale walls.

"This way, sir," Farrell announced.

Holt tensed, startled as Farrell's voice intruded on his inspection of their surroundings. "Is there an office?"

"There is, but perhaps you'd like a chance to rest and have a meal?"

"No, thank you. I'm only here to inspect the property. I'll leave my case in the office, then you can show me around."

Farrell's mask of noble servitude cracked for just an instant, the line of a frown appearing between his brows, just as quickly smoothed away. Holt wondered what about his request disturbed the man.

"Very well," Farrell replied evenly and then gestured toward the closed doors. "In there." The doors glided open soundlessly at Farrell's touch. He waved Holt forward with an open hand.

Holt let his gaze rove over the space before he entered. Sheer curtains softened the shaft of sunlight piercing a part of the gloom. A heavy desk centered on an ornate oriental rug in shades of red and gold dominated the side of the room nearest the window. Dark paneled walls and heavy green velvet drapery on the large, single window created a deep sense of quiet.

Opposite the window, a wide wall unit stood, doors open. Snug black pants-clad legs extended from inside onto the floor, then to crossed ankles and the soles of narrow shoes. The rest of her, for Holt was certain only a woman could boast those delicate ankles, was on hands and knees inspecting something inside the cabinet. He cleared his throat.

The woman's torso jerked upward. A thunk, followed by a mostly unintelligible string of epithets in an otherwise charming accent, filled the air. She backed out of the cabinet, pert rear then curved hips, a tiny waist, and finally the rest of her on knees and one hand gripping a small flashlight, the other hand rubbing the back of her head. The gloom left Holt wondering if her hair was brown or auburn. As pale as her skin appeared, he decided it must be auburn.

"Your pardon, miss," Farrell intoned from behind him.

"Farrell, how many times do I have to tell ye, dinna sneak up on a lass like that?" she complained as she turned, saw Holt and shifted her hand from the back of her head to her mouth. "Oops, sorry."

Her comment to Farrell and her position in the cabinet suggested to Holt she was from a cleaning service the estate used. "And you are?" Holt kept his expression neutral, but it took effort. The view from the front was enticing, too. Large dark brown eyes in a perfect oval face, fair skin, dark auburn hair in a disarrayed pixie cut, and a chest designed to counterbalance her nicely curved bottom half. But her expression was so chagrined, he had to stifle a laugh. He saw no reason to embarrass her further.

"Caitlin Paterson," she replied from behind her hand then dropped it to her side. "And ye are?"

"This is Mr. Holt Ridley," Farrell announced from behind Holt's shoulder. "The heir. Mr. Ridley, your appraiser."

"Ach, I thought I'd have more time," Ms. Paterson muttered under her breath, half turning to glance back toward the wall unit she'd just exited, then casting a narrow gaze on Farrell.

Holt was certain she hadn't meant for that comment to be overheard either because she colored when her gaze moved from Farrell to him, and she saw the quirk of his lips. "Interesting to meet you," he chided with a glance toward the floor of the open cabinet, then back to the roses staining Ms. Paterson's ivory skin.

This was the expert antique appraiser the lawyer had promised to make a full and complete assessment of the contents of this overblown mausoleum?

"Sorry. I was looking for a maker's mark in…well, I have no' found it yet." She shoved the small flashlight into a back pocket.

Holt's body reacted to the idea of that pert rear under his own hand.

"You will have to continue your search later, Miss Caitlin," Farrell interjected. "Mr. Ridley has need of the office."

She huffed and planted her fists on her hips, then, with the heir in the room, must have thought better of arguing. She turned and closed the cabinet door. "Let me know when ye are done if ye will," she requested and with a nod to each, strode past them and out the door.

"Young, isn't she? Yet she's the appraiser?" Holt couldn't wait to hear how Miss Caitlin had developed her expertise.

"The very same," Farrell replied. "She comes highly recommended."

Holt thought about the view he'd gotten when he first saw the room and decided highly recommended didn't begin to describe her.

CHAPTER 2

Long before the end of the day, Holt became convinced his notion of a quick return to California was a lost cause. The house was too big, contained too many valuable things mixed with utter beachy *kitsch*, and needed too much work for him to be able to manage the estate contents and real estate sale from a distance. And if he didn't stay, he'd have to return next week anyway to answer the damned summons. He texted his assistant to pack a week's worth of cold weather clothing in two suitcases and overnight them to him. He always slept raw, so the lack of anything to wear tonight didn't bother him. He could live in what he had on his back and in his go-bag long enough for two boxes to arrive. He'd managed with less.

He leaned back from the desk where he'd settled after touring the house to study the papers the lawyer had left with him. The room had darkened around the pool of lamplight while he read. Days were short this far north this time of year. He rang for Farrell, who appeared so quickly, Holt figured he'd been hovering outside the office door. "I'll be here for a week— possibly as much as ten days. Which room should I use?"

"For the holiday, sir, would you like us to decorate the house, then?"

Holt snorted. "Not on my account."

Farrell nodded. "Follow me if you're ready. I've had the master suite prepared in the event you'd remain with us overnight."

He should have expected that. "Not there. Are my mother's old rooms available?"

"Apologies, sir, but Miss Caitlin is currently using that suite."

He didn't bother to ask what was behind Farrell's hesitation. Miss Caitlin had quickly made herself at home, it seemed.

The master suite loomed large in his imagination. If Holt were a superstitious man, the idea of sleeping in his evil great-aunt's bed would give him nightmares. He shook off the feeling. He wasn't a child. "Very well, lead the way."

The master suite was as ostentatious as the rest of the house. The heavy furniture and draperies didn't surprise him. Nor did the plumbing in the master bath, barely modernized to early twentieth-century standards. It had the look of old-fashioned luxury but lacked twenty-first-century amenities. Still, it was better than what he'd grown up with. It would have to do.

"Your great-aunt had many of the rooms updated, baths included, but preferred her own as you find it,"

Farrell told him. "The bedding, of course, has been changed, and we will acquire any toiletries you prefer. I hope you will be comfortable here." He put Holt's go-bag on the brocade-covered padded bench at the end of the bed.

Holt had slept in worse surroundings. "Thank you."

Farrell went to the door, then paused. "Make yourself at home. Dinner will be ready in thirty minutes. I'll escort you—"

"I can find my way to the dining room."

"The small dining room, if you please, sir." Farrell nodded and left him alone.

Holt unpacked his go-bag and hung up his spare pants and shirt, then wandered around the room, picking up and replacing objects without really seeing them. He tried to recall details of the house's main floor Farrell had shown him, but they blurred together into a montage of walnut paneling, colorful carpets, and beveled glass.

The master bedroom windows looked out over the back garden to the ocean, but night had fallen quickly, hiding the view. He stared out into the darkness for a moment, then checked his watch and realized he was going to be late. His stomach should still be on California time, where it was mid-afternoon, but perhaps refusing the meal and taking the tour immediately after a sleepless night coming cross-country had not been his best idea. Now that he was alone, he realized he was hungry as well as tired. He supposed a meal would help him adjust to the local time. He pictured the route to the small dining room as he headed out the door, then his mind turned to a potentially more pleasant matter. Would Caitlin Paterson be at dinner, too?

~

Caitlin entered the small dining room. Candlelight replaced the expected glow of the overhead chandelier. She noticed the second place setting at the head of the table and supposed that was the reason for the mood lighting. The new master was on the premises. No doubt, the staff wanted to make a good first impression. Not that she thought of Farrell and Mrs. Smith as mere staff. They'd been kind to her, and they cared for this place as if it was their own. They were special people. She hoped Ridley came to see them the way she did and took care of them, whatever he decided to do with the estate.

She took her usual seat at the side of the long table which, over her objections, Farrell had insisted she use for her meals. At least they hadn't insisted on using the formal dining room, easily three times the size of this one. She should count her blessings, but she would've been more comfortable eating in the kitchen than out here by herself. Well, she wouldn't be eating by herself tonight, would she? The laird of the manor had arrived.

She'd been so embarrassed by the way he'd found her, she'd kept her gaze down and barely recalled what he'd looked like. Tall, dark hair, athletic build, that was the sum of the impression she'd gotten as she hastened out of the office. She never looked at his face. What must he think of her?

Mr. Holt Ridley, billionaire heir to all of this, must have had quite a view— her with her head in the cabinet and her *arse* in the air. The thought made her blush, even now. She'd closed those pocket doors for a reason, damn it. But she couldn't fault Farrell, not with the laird demanding entrance.

She dreaded their second meeting. What would she *say* to the man? Worse, what would he say to her? As far as he knew, she was just part of the hired help. Would he object to sharing the table with her? That thought didn't bother her as much as she knew it should. Still, she would happily escape to the kitchen or her chamber, if she could.

She didn't have to wait long to find out. Holt Ridley strode in as if he owned the place— in fact, he did— shoulders back, step assured, and not the least bit hesitant. Caitlin envied him that. Good looking, even more so now that he'd abandoned his suit jacket. Even features, chiseled jaw, his chin was neither too strong nor too weak; Holt Ridley's looks appealed to her.

And that was a problem. She knew better than to get involved with the boss. Yet the white shirt he wore stretched over impressively broad shoulders. He'd also rolled the sleeves up his forearms since she'd seen him last, drawing her attention to his broad, tanned hands. Nice. Did he do any real work with them or just buy and sell, and count his money?

"Good evening." She took the initiative rather than let him control their conversation from the start. She wouldn't let him put her on the spot like he had in the office.

His stride broke ever so slightly. Had she glanced away, she never would have seen it. So he could be put off-kilter, eh?

"Good evening." He met her gaze with eyes the color of stone, gray and hard, and took his seat. He frowned at the serviette on his plate, picked it up and shook it out, then draped it across his lap. "Is this usual?" He waved a hand.

Caitlin had no difficulty taking his meaning. He'd indicated the table setting and the small but formal dining room around them. "Somewhat." She shrugged. "I've been eating alone in here the past two days. Though usually by the light of the chandelier," she told him and gestured toward it. "The candlelight is a bit…spooky, actually."

His gaze dropped from the light fixture to her. "Not the romantic sort, then, are you?"

Sarcasm seemed to be his weapon of choice. *Interesting to meet her—* her arse. Caitlin opened her mouth, intending to return fire. Fortunately, Farrell and Mrs. Smith came in bearing silver-domed plates, set them down in perfect synchrony, and lifted the domes away. The scent of their dinner wafting past her nose made Caitlin's mouth water. No matter what else might aggravate her while staying here, she could not complain about the food. Tonight's menu included poached salmon with dill, a potato casserole of some sort and bright green peas. Melted butter drenched a split roll, soft and still steaming from the oven. She smiled her thanks to Mrs. Smith as Farrell approached with a bottle.

"Wine, miss? It's a local vintage, from a north fork estate."

"Thank you, I believe I will." If Mr. Ridley intended to be a disagreeable dinner companion, maybe some wine would loosen him up enough for them to have a civil conversation. At the very least, a glass or two would make her feel better about it if he didn't.

Farrell poured for them both, then set the bottle in a crystal dish near Ridley, and left the room.

After a moment, she realized Ridley was waiting for her to start. Decided to be polite, had he? She picked up her fork and sampled the fish, which melted in her mouth. A taste of the potato casserole and she forgot her dinner companion for as long as it took to savor the creamy, cheesy richness. She hoped her eyes hadn't rolled back in her head. She hadn't groaned in appreciation, had she? She snuck a glance Ridley's way. His gaze was on the piece of bread he was using to sop up more of the melted butter, but a small smile played around his lips. Damn, she had.

"It's rather good, aye?" she asked, to cover her embarrassment.

"Indeed. Irish butter, I believe."

"What?" She meant the fish and the potato casserole. "How would ye ken…I mean *know*…?"

"Oh, we're quite civilized in California. All the latest food fads either start or end up there. Irish butter has been popular for months."

"No' in Scotland," she muttered and tried a bite of the butter-soaked bread. She wouldn't admit it tasted quite good.

"You're Scottish, then?" He took a bite of potato casserole.

Caitlin grinned as his eyes closed with obvious pleasure. So, he had a bit of a hedonistic streak, too, alongside that sarcastic wit he'd displayed since she first met him. You'd think a billionaire who could have anything he wanted any time he wanted it would have gotten blasé about such simple pleasures as a cheesy potato casserole or imported butter. Caitlin found herself wondering what else would make his dark eyes close in appreciation.

Nay! No sense wondering about that. She was here to do a job, then return to Scotland. Ridley was here for a few days before he headed home to California, and she'd never see him again.

"Aye, I'm from Scotland," she told him as his eyes opened. She dropped her gaze quickly to her plate, pretending she hadn't noticed his lapse, though she couldn't say why she did him that favor. She distracted herself by wondering if he knew her cousin's wife's family in California. That would be proof of a small world indeed.

"So, the estate lawyer thought the things in this house were British imports. That is the reason you were hired?"

Caitlin took the question as a challenge. "Aye, and for the most part, they are. He has documentation on some of it, bills of lading and whatnot, from when they were shipped from England, some recent, some going back many decades or longer. I've experience with many types of British antiques, most recently with pieces from the Jacobite period."

"Which is…?"

"Eighteenth-century. 'Tis a long, sad tale. I'd sooner no' spoil our dinner in the telling. Some other time."

A small frown drew his brows together, forming that crease she'd noticed earlier.

"And your recent expertise with Jaco...what did you call it?"

"Jacobite. Whether any of the pieces in this house are Jacobite remains to be seen." Even if she knew, she didn't see the sense in telling the man over dinner that his ancestors had stolen some of the contents of this house from her ancestors, at best after forcing them from their homes and land. At worst, they had killed the men and bairns, then raped and killed the women. He wouldn't consider that proper dinner conversation.

"When do you think you'll...see?"

"I've only started, really. This could take weeks, perhaps months, to reliably determine the provenance of some furnishings."

"Months...?" He set his fork aside. "I mean to sell this mausoleum as soon as possible. You'll have to work faster than that."

Sell this fabulous place? Was he out of his mind? "I'll do the best I can, but research can take time. Perhaps after you have been here a few days, you'll better appreciate what you have inherited."

He set his jaw in a grim line. "Only for what it's worth. I have no sentimental attachment to anything on this property. Quite the opposite."

And didn't that sound ominous? Caitlin returned her attention to her plate. Her dinner companion had nothing good to share. Her food, at least, she could enjoy.

Holt grimaced, certain that Caitlin, who had quickly dropped her gaze and failed to comment, had taken offense. She obviously loved old things, or she wouldn't do the work she did. No doubt she had already fallen in love with many things here. He glanced around the room and hid a smile. That could work to his advantage. She'd naturally assign greater monetary value to things she admired.

Still, he pressed his lips together, fighting to keep from challenging her silence. It would do her no good to become attached to the house or anything in it. He intended to get rid of it all and never set foot on Long Island again, except as required to pass through JFK. The sooner she finished the job she'd been hired to do, the better.

Assuming, of course, that his lawyers could break his great-aunt's will and eliminate the stipulation that he live here before selling the place. He could barely tolerate the idea of spending one night under this roof, much less ninety of them.

The thought crossed his mind that he could simply fire Ms. Paterson and get on with the sale. But no, he needed her to do her job. His company could use the infusion of cash, and if the contents were valuable in their own right, so much the better.

He took a sip of the wine Farrell poured and found it acceptable. Caitlin hadn't touched hers yet. He tipped the bottle in her direction. "Would you prefer something else?"

Absently, Caitlin sipped her wine, then shook her head. "Nay, this will do nicely."

He set the bottle aside. "I thought people mostly drank tea and whisky in Scotland."

She settled back in her chair and eyed him.

Though he found her quite attractive, he didn't enjoy her scrutiny quite as much as he'd expected.

"We do," she bit out, "but we also drink coffee and wine. And we have the best water in the world." She took a larger sip from her glass, then straightened. "I take it ye have never been to Scotland?"

"No, never needed to." He took a bite of fish, his gaze meeting hers as he chewed. She had a glint in her eye. Apparently, he'd said something wrong— again.

"Never needed to? You don't go on holiday?" Caitlin frowned.

Holt picked up his wine glass, then set it aside. "Vacation? I don't have time. If I travel, it's for work, though I conduct most of my meetings by teleconference. I'm here only because I'm legally required to be in order to settle the estate."

She set her fork on her plate, her disbelieving gaze on him. "So to you, this trip is nothing but business."

"Yes. What else would it be?"

"A chance to reclaim part of your heritage? To meet long-lost relatives who might still live in the area?" She leaned forward and waved a hand. "To enjoy the holidays away from your all-consuming work? I can think of many reasons why you could enjoy this visit." She raised her glass as if in salute, or to punctuate her point, and took a long drink.

"Then you'd be wrong." He would not let himself focus on the way her lips pressed the rim of the glass in her hand or how her throat moved as she swallowed. She seemed bent on irritating him this evening. Rather than becoming consumed with that mouth, that throat, he would go with her attitude. He emptied his glass and poured another. The bottle was getting low. "More wine?" He tipped the bottle toward her glass.

Her shoulders tensed. "No, thank you. And while we're on the subject of the reason for your visit, how can you call this estate a mausoleum? There's much to appreciate here. The beautiful furnishings, the history of the house and property, the setting. Yet, you just want to be rid of it. You Americans have no sense of history. Everything has to be clean and new, aye? I can imagine how your place in California is furnished— chrome and glass minimalism? Am I close?"

She frowned when he didn't respond, but her comments hit too close to home. Not so much chrome and glass, but minimalism, certainly. He spent so much time at work, he'd done little to make a home for himself. His condo was a place to sleep and not much more until Helen Conroe threw herself at him. Now, he was back to sleeping alone, and let that be a lesson to him.

"I hope I can open your eyes before you make a huge mistake here." Caitlin gestured with her half-full glass.

Her assessment made him uncomfortable, and that made him fight back. How much did she know about his family history? And him? He kept his hands on the table, one by his plate and one toying with the wine glass's stem. Snapping it would show her that her analysis hit close to the bone, so he set it aside. "My eyes are as open as they need to be," Holt replied, on the defensive and not liking it one bit. "I don't need your help, except to do the job you're being paid to do. That doesn't include meddling in my personal life."

"I see." She laid her napkin by her plate and stood. "I think I've quite lost my appetite. I'll bid you goodnight."

Holt watched, frowning, as she left the dining room without another word. So, she didn't like being criticized, did she? Then she'd better stop trying to analyze him and do the job that the estate— his estate— was paying her to do.

CHAPTER 3

The next morning, Caitlin hurried down the village street, eager to reach the shelter of the shops in the blocks ahead. The estate's housekeeper and cook, Mrs. Smith, had suggested having a look at the nearby village as a way to combat Caitlin's lingering jet lag. She planned to get some shopping done for Hogmanay, which, rather than Christmas, was the holiday when most Scots exchanged gifts.

She also thought some time away from the estate would make a great diversion from her annoyance with Holt Ridley. He hadn't appeared before she left— still sleeping on California time, she supposed.

It was never a good idea to lash out at the person paying you. He clearly thought she'd overstepped last night. And, truth be told, she had. Normally, she might think that if she had to meddle to save the estate, she'd gladly do it again, but not if it meant losing this job. A good reference from Ridley would have too great an impact on the future she hoped to have. Getting out of his way for a few hours this morning seemed a brilliant idea.

But Caitlin hadn't counted on the weather changing as fast as it did in Scotland. She'd left her coat at the estate, and the lightweight wool jumper she had on wasn't quite up to the task. This morning, the wind blowing down the Long Island Sound from the north was as damp and chill as the wind howling across a Highland loch in winter. It didn't make her homesick— quite. She preferred lovely spring days, warm blue skies, and the scent of bluebells in the woods, but she could get through the rest of this month knowing by spring, she'd be home and perhaps even in the job she wanted.

All the holiday decorations missing from the mansion must have been loaned to the village, she thought as she neared her objective. Shop windows were festooned with red and green garlands, bows, and wreaths. Pillar candles, mostly lit by tea lights, lent a warm glow to the shady side of the street. A large fir tree in the central square ahead was covered in lights she expected would be festive after dark, along with more ornaments than she could count, garland and more bows.

She spotted her first destination in the next block and picked up her pace, eager to get out of the wind. She wanted to find something from America her cousin's twins would enjoy. She should have chosen a closer parking space on the street, but Farrell had warned she couldn't count on those being available and had set the village car park a block behind the shops into the car's GPS.

She passed a cluster of people who smiled, acknowledging her, then a few who ignored her except as an obstacle to be avoided. She supposed they were on their way to work. The sidewalk emptied after she passed them, and the scent of cinnamon and baking bread reached her. Tea and a scone suddenly sounded enticing. Did they have scones here?

Before she knew what was happening, a sharp tug on her shoulder strap spun her around. She held on as a young man tried to wrestle her purse away from her. "What do ye think ye're doing? Let go of that," she barked.

Despite using her elbows to defend herself, she was losing ground. Her attacker grabbed her wrist, trying to break her hold. He had almost gotten the strap away from her when a tall, dark-haired man yanked the would-be thief aside. Her attacker let go of her purse strap and fell back, swearing as the man spun him about, shoved him face-first against the bricks of a shop wall, and held him there with a solid grip on his neck and a well-muscled arm across his shoulders.

"Are you all right, miss?" the stranger asked, glancing with steel-blue eyes from Caitlin's attacker to her and back again.

She took a quick inventory. She'd have a few bruises tomorrow along with a scrape on her hand from the buckle of the purse strap, but other than that, she was fine. "No permanent harm done," she reported. "What are ye going to do with him?"

"Nothing." The man tipped his head to indicate the police car rolling down the street in their direction. "I knew someone would call the cops. Your friend here obviously thought the street was empty." He shifted his grip as the thief tried to break his hold. "Stand still. You seem to have forgotten in a small town like this, someone is always watching."

After a few more minutes of standing in the cold while the deputy locked the thief in the back of his car then took their brief statements, Caitlin finally had the chance to thank her rescuer. "I'm Caitlin Paterson. That deputy called you Doc," she continued as the car pulled away. "Are you a medical doctor?" He had a few glints of silver at his temples to go with his confident manner, making her guess he was in his late forties or early fifties.

"Veterinarian," he reported. "Jim Coates at your service. From your accent, I'd say you're not from around here."

She gave a rueful laugh. "I'm from Scotland. I arrived three days ago." With a glance toward the retreating car, she added, "No' the welcome I expected."

His gaze followed hers toward the police car as it pulled away. "Hell of an introduction to the village. Sorry about that." He shook his head, then turned back to her. "I've been to Scotland. A few years ago. Beautiful place."

"Thank you. Look, I owe you for today. Can I at least buy you a cup of coffee?"

"I'll have to take a rain check. I'm late for my first appointment. But I'd enjoy talking to you about Scotland sometime." His gaze dropped to her hand, and he frowned. "Still, you might want to get that cut looked at."

"Nay, 'tis just a scratch. But I'd love to hear about your trip. Of course, another time will do. I'm so sorry to have made ye late."

Dr. Coates nodded what she took for his agreement. As she watched him turn at the first side street and disappear, a woman joined her on the sidewalk.

"Hello, I'm Alice Nash. I saw the constable's car leaving from my shop." She gestured to the bakery Caitlin had scented just before she'd been accosted. "You must be shaken up. Why don't you come with me? I'll make you something hot to drink."

Caitlin nodded, overwhelmed by the woman's sympathetic tone. After the last half hour, Caitlin needed to sit and unwind. She'd thaw out for a few minutes, let her hands stop shaking, then return to her car and head back to the estate. Shopping could wait for another day.

A cheerful jingle from the brass doorbell announced their entry. Caitlin paused just inside the door for a moment to take a breath and let her face warm. Delightful scents of bread, sugar, and spices filled the air.

Alice kept going, then paused and turned around to face her. "Have a seat and get off your feet for a few minutes. What would you like? On the house."

Caitlin judged Alice to be in her mid-forties, but she had a timeless motherly air, reinforced by her generous offer. "On the…oh, thank you. That's no' necessary."

"Nonsense. My treat," Alice insisted.

Caitlin relented. "Tea would be wonderful. Milk and sugar. And do ye have any scones?"

Alice grinned. "Probably not like you're used to, but try one and tell me what you think." She waved, indicating the bakery's interior. "Sit anywhere. I'll bring everything to you." She leaned a hand on the counter and waited for Caitlin to make up her mind.

Caitlin sank into a chair at the nearest cafe table and let herself breathe. Last evening's argument with Holt Ridley and this morning's events were not an auspicious start to her trip. She watched Alice bustle around behind the counter while telling herself to stop the nonsense. She sounded like her granny. The guy had only tried to grab her purse. She wasn't hurt, not seriously. She still had her belongings, and she'd met a knight in shining armor who might, with his recollections of his time in Scotland, ease her homesickness a wee bit, and a friendly baker who offered her the comfort of a warm cup of tea and a scone. On balance, the morning was turning out more positive than negative. Jet lag had to be what was making her shaky.

In moments, Alice brought a tray with a proper teapot and all the trimmings, three small, triangular scones, jam, and whipped cream.

"I made an assumption from your accent," she said with a nod toward the small bowl of cream. "I don't have any clotted cream, so I hope this will do. With the strawberry jam, right? It's all local, from nearby farms."

"It's lovely. You're too generous."

"Nonsense. You've had a rough morning. Are you hurt anywhere?"

Caitlin stirred sugar into her tea, then added a splash of milk, keeping her scratched hand in her lap. "Nay." She took a sip and let the warmth thaw her all the way down and steady her nerves. Then, while she loaded one of the scones with cream and jam, she gave Alice the full story of the drama she'd just missed.

"Oh, no! How could something like that happen, right here on the square, and in broad daylight? I'm so sorry." Alice glanced down at Caitlin's hand. "And you *are* hurt!"

"Not much. A scratch."

"Let me get my first-aid kit, and we'll take care of it."

Caitlin suspected she'd waste her breath if she tried to argue. Instead, while Alice fetched her supplies from behind her counter, she sampled the scone she'd prepared and groaned at the buttery goodness and the bright, sweet strawberry jam. "These are brilliant!" After another bite, she asked, "What do you know about the veterinarian who helped me? He said his name is Jim Coates."

"He's fairly new in town," Alice replied from the counter while sorting through the first-aid kit's contents. "Quiet and keeps to himself when not at his office. Ah, here we go." She returned with a tube of ointment and a bandage. "Antibacterial," she explained as she dabbed some greasy-looking ointment on the gauze, then gestured for Caitlin to hold out her hand. "Maybe two years ago he opened his practice. Pets mostly, and a few farm animals. He trains service dogs. Or rescue dogs. Something like that."

Scratch duly covered, Caitlin thanked her, then continued, "I promised him a coffee for coming to my rescue today."

"Good luck making that happen. So far, I hear he hasn't been the social sort. All work and no play…" Alice got up and returned to the counter to put away her supplies, then asked, "Where are you staying?"

"At Hampton Dales. I'm appraising the estate's contents."

"Oh, well, that must be interesting. I haven't been in town long, myself, but I've already heard the place is haunted or unlucky in some way. Everyone is vague. You know how rumors spread."

Caitlin nodded, intrigued. "In bits and bobs, aye. So that's all you know?"

Alice shrugged as the bell over the door jangled. The news about Caitlin's incident had obviously spread. Several people, many of them nearby shopkeepers, stopped by to express their regret for her trouble and ask about her welfare. The attention embarrassed her, but Alice helped her with names and filled her in about each person after they left. Caitlin resolved not to share any of her own secrets with the chatty baker. No telling what she'd pass along.

Full of comfort food and ears ringing from Alice's tales, Caitlin bid her new friend goodbye. She'd recovered enough to visit a nearby shop Alice recommended. It was a treasure-trove. A wonderland for kids of all ages. When she spotted a section of vintage board games, she knew she'd come to the right place. Ian and Lara's twins loved word games. She found Scrabble in several languages and bought one in English and one in German. The twins would have fun with all those long, compound German nouns. Satisfied, she headed back to the estate, this time without being accosted.

After returning the car keys to Farrell and telling him about her adventure in the village, Caitlin decided the best way to put the mugging out of her mind was to lose herself in her work. She entered the estate's beautiful walnut, bookshelf-lined library and looked around, bemused. How could Ridley not see what she saw in this house? She ran a cotton-gloved hand over the smooth wood and traced a bit of wainscoting with one finger. Either it had been well taken care of or lovingly restored. Shelves to the barrel-vaulted ceiling were filled with books. Old leather-bound tomes, encyclopedias, medical books, everything to satisfy a curious mind, including paperback romance, mystery, science fiction novels, and children's books. Had Ridley lived here as a child and read those? Somehow, their presence added a more human scale to the otherwise important space.

She turned full circle, overwhelmed by the sheer challenge of this room. One more thing for her to-do list. She must find a librarian who could evaluate all these books. Or she could simply include the library as a whole in her catalog and assign it some fantastic value. Certainly, many of these books were costly, though many were clearly not valuable, except, perhaps, to a collector.

Another crystal chandelier sparkled in the center of the ceiling's vault. There would be a record of its purchase somewhere. At least there weren't any paintings to evaluate in here— the bookcases took up nearly every bit of wall space. Sconces above wainscoting took the rest.

She continued her inspection, crawling under the library table to determine its pedigree, overturning chairs and finally, approaching a massive globe in its protective stand. It didn't take an expert to see the globe's continents and seas were made of semi-precious stone. Old borders and capitals were picked out in precious gems and identified in etched, flowing, hand-inked script. The entire piece was breathtaking, possibly priceless, and belonged in a museum. Judging by some of the country names and borders, it had to be at least two hundred years old. Gently, she turned the globe, eager to see more of it. If she could determine its provenance, she could go online and find out more about it. Were there any more like it in the world? She'd never seen a globe so beautifully made.

And Holt Ridley wanted to discard it and everything else in this estate. She shook her head. The man was *barmy*. What would it take to get through to him? To make him see what he had here? Was he so much a product of this century that he could not appreciate beautiful things from the past?

Why did he hate this place so much that he couldn't wait to be rid of it? All of those were questions she'd love to get answers to but were probably none of her business. Still, if she could somehow make him see what she saw, perhaps he wouldn't be so eager to sell.

∽

Holt found Caitlin in the estate's library, notepad on the table in front of her and pen in hand, a camera beside a pair of white cotton gloves nearby. The thoughtful expression on her face as she wrote made her seem worlds away, and, given the way her gaze kept shifting to a globe in a stand near her chair, perhaps she was.

He didn't want to disturb her work, but he owed her an apology for the way he behaved at dinner last night. He crossed his arms, leaned against the doorframe and then scuffed his shoe on the parquet floor.

Her gaze tracked around the room until it landed on him. "Hiya. I thought I heard something."

"I didn't want to startle you."

She studied him for a moment before she spoke. "Are you checking up on me?"

Holt waved a hand. "No. I came to apologize for last night. I shouldn't have been such a jerk."

"A jerk?"

Did they use the word in Scotland? "Yes. My only excuse is jet lag. I took the red-eye to get here yesterday morning."

"I see."

Despite her clipped replies, she seemed to be taking this well. She wasn't frowning at him, at least. Holt decided to try a little charm. "So, am I forgiven?"

Caitlin set aside her writing materials and stood. "Mr. Ridley, you— or your solicitor— hired me to do a job. I'm doing it," she added with a wave of her hand, then crossed her arms. "What you do with your estate once I finish is up to you." A quick frown drew a line between her brows, then smoothed away, as if she decided it wasn't in her best interest to pick a fight with him.

Still, he was clearly not forgiven. "As true as that is, I'd still like us not to be at odds while you're here. Why don't we start by using first names? I'm Holt."

"Do names matter? Either way, I'll do what I was hired to do."

Frustrated, Holt cast about for a way to keep his apology from turning into another argument. Appealing to her expertise seemed to be the best way to deflect this uncomfortable conversation. "What are you working on?"

"This globe. I'm making notes, then I'll use the pictures I've taken to do some further research on it."

"Why? It looks like any other globe to me."

"Come closer." She beckoned, then pulled on the gloves.

Holt straightened and went where she directed him. "It's pretty, I'll give you that."

"As well you should. But it's more than pretty." She gave it a gentle spin and pointed out the features that made it special, from the quality of the stones and the artistry of its construction to the historical place names and boundaries.

He'd also noted the bandage on her hand and wondered how she'd hurt it. But she didn't mention it, and since her gloves hid it, he soon forgot to ask. She clearly knew her subject, and her enthusiasm for it succeeded where her proclamations at dinner last night had not. Holt's interest was piqued. "Okay, I'll admit, it's an attractive and thought-provoking piece." He could say the same about her. Attractive and thought-provoking. And irritating.

"And if my suspicion is correct, it's unique enough to be the perfect cover image for the catalog of the estate's furnishings that I'll put together for the auction."

Holt nodded. She hadn't liked his comment last night, but it appeared she'd taken it on board. "Thank you."

"No need to thank me. I'm just doing what I was hired to do." She pulled off the gloves. "If that's all…?"

Dismissing him, was she? "Not entirely. I'd like to get a sense of the age and condition of the estate's furnishings. Not in detail, just your general impression. What can you tell me so far?"

Caitlin frowned but resumed her seat and gestured him to one on the other side of the table. "Farrell and Mrs. Smith have done an excellent job maintaining the contents of the estate. It has helped, I suppose, that no young children have resided here in a generation."

"Who told you that?"

"Mrs. Smith, of course. The house is not, as you say, child-proof. I understand from her that your mother was the latest, and she was in high school during her residence."

Holt's belly clenched as he pictured his mother living in this house under her aunt's thumb. Her parents had died in a car crash early in her sophomore year in high school, and with no other relatives, she'd wound up dependent on her widowed aunt's begrudged charity.

"For a little over three years, yes." Holt considered telling her how his mother had been forced to work two jobs to support them, but hadn't he told Caitlin, just last night, that her responsibilities didn't include meddling in his personal life?

As she filled him in on what she'd gleaned so far, ticking off points on her fingertips, Holt understood how she'd won this job. In her professional element, her intellect and expertise were undeniable. He'd been attracted to her beauty at first, but her smarts made her even more intriguing. And that was a problem. Helen Conroe had taught him not to get too close to someone in a professional relationship, not to trust their motives. He needed to remember that and keep Ms. Paterson at arm's length.

CHAPTER 4

Caitlin finished her preliminary survey of the library the next afternoon and decided to reward herself by having a walk on the nearby beach. As she crossed the back lawn, she heard a car come up the front drive and wondered if it was Holt returning from wherever he had gone.

She hadn't spoken to him since he left her in the library the day before. He'd even skipped dinner, which worried her a bit. Had she made such a terrible impression that he was avoiding her? She'd passed the office door several times since he'd arrived and seen him hunched over his laptop, intent on his reading, fingers flying over the keyboard as he answered emails or wrote memos or whatever he did to keep his company running smoothly. Even three thousand miles away from his business and life in California, he couldn't leave them behind. One of the pitfalls of being the boss that she knew well. The only difference between his situation and hers was that she was her company. She had no one else to cause problems, and no one else to rely on. If she had to work twenty hours a day to finish a job, she did.

She continued down to the beach, where Holt surprised her, coming across the lawn behind her and calling her name.

"I saw you through the back windows," he said, stopping as soon as he reached the sand to remove his shoes and socks and roll up his pants. "Ah, warm sand, cool air. Can't beat the combination."

"And cold water?" She gestured toward the dark green water lapping at the shoreline. She had intended to wander the beach alone but decided she would make the effort to enjoy Holt's company, too. He seemed more relaxed, less stand-offish than he had the past two days. Perhaps getting away from the house was good for him.

"Probably colder than you're used to."

Caitlin kicked off her shoes and tugged off her socks, then rolled up her pants legs. "I think a highland loch would be colder than the ocean this time of year."

Holt shook his head. "I don't know…"

She heard his rising intonation as a challenge and decided to accept it. Walking into the water until it was ankle-deep, she fought to keep her expression serene. "It is cold, but nowhere near as cold as it would be in the Highlands."

Holt snorted and moved toward her. She heard the breath he sucked in as soon as his toes touched the water, but he kept going, reaching her and passing until the surge hit just below his knees. "The tide's coming in. The deeper you go, the colder it gets."

Caitlin joined him. Holt was a few inches taller, so the water hit her legs just above the knee. "Nay. I swim in colder lochs in the summer." As soon as she finished speaking, a wave rounding the point rushed the shore and knocked her off her feet.

Caitlin came up spluttering, soaked and chilled through, her teeth chattering. It took a moment for her to realize Holt's arms were around her, holding her up. He'd gotten wet saving her, but he was marginally warmer than she, so she clung to him. He pushed her hair out of her face as she held onto him, and she caught her breath at his expression— pensive and dark. His lips were damp with sea water, full, and tempting. Would they be warm, or cold? Salty or sweet? Firm or soft? The urge to find out burst through any inhibitions she might have used to guard herself from this man. But before she could react, he scooped her up and carried her back to shore, where he put her down.

"Are you okay?"

She shivered. "I will be once we get back inside," she said as she moved up the sand. Out of Holt's embrace, the breeze deepened her chill from her dunking in cold water. Her hands shook and her teeth wanted to keep chattering, but she clenched her jaw. In a rush to collect her shoes and run back to the house to get warm, she hastened across the beach, but halfway, she stepped on something hard and sharp. With a cry, she fell flat-out, arms extended, turning her head in time to keep from getting a mouthful of sand.

She pushed up onto her knees, fighting to get her breath back through the pain of the jolt to her knees and torso. Holt reached her in seconds, took her arm and helped her the rest of the way up.

"I never said you had to fall at my feet," he teased.

Caitlin took a breath, trying to come up with a suitably snarky response. This was the version of Holt who'd mocked her in the library. Before she could speak, Holt crouched next to her.

"You're bleeding! Give me your foot. No, the other one."

"I didn't feel anything." She put a hand on his shoulder to help her balance on one foot and glanced around and down. The red staining the sand where Holt had helped her stand up surprised her.

"Probably because your foot's so cold." Holt brushed sand from her injured foot and inspected the bottom. "The cut's under the heel. The edges look clean, so maybe you stepped on a broken piece of glass." He studied the sand around them, then let go of her foot and put his hands on her hips to steady her as she lowered her toes to the sand. Then he stood. "Stay put for a second. I don't know exactly where you got cut, but I don't want you to step on anything sharp like that again."

"Um…what about you?"

"I'm tough." Holt gave her a grin, then went back to business. "I'm going to put on my shoes, grab yours, then carry you back to the house. Mrs. Smith must keep a first aid kit somewhere."

"How bad is the cut?" Caitlin did her best to ignore her reaction to Holt's unexpected grin— there was no reason why it should make her insides melt. She was too cold for that nonsense, and his moods were too changeable. Instead, she turned her foot from side to side, but she could only see bloody sand, not the cut. Stymied, she brushed at the sand coating the front of her body from her fall. She was pretty sure Mrs. Smith wouldn't appreciate her bringing half the beach into the house with her.

"I don't think it needs stitches." Holt stepped up onto the grassy verge, swept sand from his feet with his socks, shook them out and pocketed them, then slipped on his shoes. "But you'll need to let it heal before you run your next marathon."

"No problem then. I don't have one scheduled until….oh, never."

He stepped back down onto the sand and handed her shoes to her. "Okay, up you go." He bent and scooped her up before she had time to object that she could probably wrap the injury in her socks and walk on the toes of that foot.

Secure in his arms, Caitlin decided she'd keep her mouth shut. Being snuggled against his body, warmed by his heat, was worth a small cut on her foot. She couldn't believe stand-offish Holt taking care of her like this. "Do you often rescue damsels in distress?"

He snorted and shrugged off her question. But he held her close and gazed at her, pupils dilated and expression heated in a way she couldn't mistake. His hand warmed her back as he carried her toward the house. His lips, slightly parted, tempted her again.

Then he looked away. "I don't often get the opportunity. Women nowadays want to rescue themselves."

Another reason to be glad she hadn't insisted on walking.

"I'd think you'd have lasses throwing themselves at your feet, a big, strong, handsome lad like you." Flustered, Caitlin couldn't believe she'd just said that, though Holt had said it first, teasing her. But he was giving her that look again, so maybe making a fool of herself had been worth it. "I'm sorry I was so clumsy," she added, hoping to restore some semblance of her dignity. Yet, that look in his eye told her he wanted her.

"You weren't clumsy. You were unlucky."

So, he was ignoring her description of him. Maybe he thought she was making fun of him. But she'd meant every word. Especially now that she was this close to him, with the muscles of his arms burning into her back and the backs of her thighs, one hand curled around her leg, the other holding her against his chest. She lifted her hand, wrapped it around his neck and tunneled her fingers into his hair, telling herself she only meant to warm them. When he leaned his head back into her palm, Caitlin traced his cheek with her other hand. "Thank you."

"Not necessary. You'd have done the same for me."

"Well, except for the carrying you to the house part, I suppose."

Holt laughed at that, his chest vibrating against her ribs, eyes sparkling with mirth and teeth flashing white behind his full lips. "You're a resourceful woman. You'd have thought of something." He stepped up onto the back porch. "Can you get the door?"

Caitlin managed to twist the knob and open the door, surprised. This was a very different Holt Ridley than the one she'd dealt with the last two days.

Holt used his shoulder to widen the opening far enough that he could carry her inside. With his foot, he hooked a chair away from the kitchen table then set her down.

"Cross your leg and prop your foot up," he told her, then turned away. While his back was turned to close the door they'd used, Caitlin shivered, missing his body heat, and watched him move around the kitchen. His wet clothes clung to him in intriguing— and revealing— ways, confirming the sense she'd gotten in his arms that Holt was more muscular than he might appear.

"Any idea where Mrs. Smith would keep emergency supplies?" Holt started pulling open drawers, stretching his wet shirt across his back and shoulders, the sleeves clinging to the muscles of his arms. She pulled her gaze away. Despite how friendly he'd seemed on the beach, and how heroic rescuing her from the waves and the cut on her foot, getting caught drooling over the man who'd hired her was a good way to lose this job.

Instead, she studied their surroundings. This had to be the cleanest kitchen she'd ever seen. The countertops were clear except for a simple white canister set. The cabinets looked old but well-kept. The window over the sink sparkled. On its sill, a small, framed picture of a young man in uniform was the only personal item Caitlin saw.

"Wait, here's a first-aid kit. Got it." He grabbed a dishtowel, wet it, sat across from her and pulled her foot and lower leg onto his thighs.

If cleaning the sand from her cut didn't hurt so much, Caitlin would have sighed at the feel of his muscle beneath her calf. Instead, she winced.

"Sorry." Holt found a tube of antiseptic ointment in the kit and smeared some on her cut, then tore open a gauze square and stuck it on top. "It stopped bleeding. All this should keep it from getting infected," he said, reaching for a tape dispenser.

"Don't bother to tape it," Caitlin told him. "I need to get cleaned up and put on some dry clothes, then I'll bandage it again."

"I'll help you."

In the shower? She bit her lip to keep from blurting out the thought. They'd met only two days ago and spent most of that time arguing. She knew better than to encourage him. Or herself.

"Thanks, but I can manage." She got up to limp to her room and took a couple of mincing steps on her toes.

"Wait." Holt scooped her up and, over her continued protests that she could manage for herself, carried her upstairs.

"Hush. I'm rescuing you again. Let me enjoy it." He paused at the door to her suite and put her down, a pained expression on his face.

"What's wrong? Did you pull something carrying me up here?" How mortifying would that be?

"No, it's not that. I…Farrell told me you were using my mother's old rooms. I've never seen them."

"Oh. I'm sorry." She opened the door. "Sorry, my things are all over but look all you want."

"I'll wait until you're not soaking wet, cold, and injured. Go on. Try to keep your foot dry."

"In the shower?" Shite, there was an image she should not have put in his head. Of course, it was probably already there. On the other hand, he hadn't reacted to her saying *look all you want* the way most guys would.

Instead, he nudged her forward into the room. "Okay, I'll re-bandage it when you're dressed." Then he pulled the door shut. With him on the outside. Damn.

~

Holt let hot water run over his body, showering off the salt and sand from his adventure at the beach with Caitlin. He didn't need the heat. Holding Caitlin had warmed him entirely too well, though she hadn't seemed to notice how holding her soft curves had hardened him.

He turned off the hot water and clenched his muscles as a blast of cold hit his chest and belly. It was not quite as cold as the wave that knocked her down and soaked him, but it did the job.

When he hauled her up, he'd been shocked by more than the cold. She fit against him so well. That contact made him hungry for her in a way he knew was trouble. Picking her up, holding her against his chest, feeling her fingers in his hair and her palm cupping the back of his head, her gentle touch on his cheek, he would stand in cold water for hours for the chance to feel that again and to see the way she looked at him in that moment. His face must have given away his desire, but hers did, too.

It was way too soon for them to go there. He would be foolish to think there could be anything more than infatuation between them. Not this fast, and not the way they argued. But touching her reinforced the attraction he'd felt for her the first time he'd seen her pert rear backing out of the cabinet in the office. The attraction that had kept him away from her for the last twenty-four hours. He should have continued to keep his distance instead of joining her on the beach.

Still, Caitlin Paterson fit against him as if she belonged in his arms. And because they were both here for only a short time, there was no danger of the kind of entanglement Helen had woven around him into his business affairs. Helen had made him miserable and put his company at risk. Damn her for spoiling any chance he had at trusting another woman. If she hadn't gone after his company, he could have moved on from their breakup and put her out of his mind. But her betrayal would stay with him for a long time. He should have expected it. It was just another betrayal in a long list of them, starting with his absent father and moving on to his great-aunt's treatment of his mother and him. But Helen had caught him by surprise, nonetheless.

He ducked his head under the spray, then shoved his hair back and scrubbed cold drops of water from his face. As near as he could tell, Caitlin was no Helen. And Scotland— where Caitlin was headed as soon as she finished the job she'd come here to do— was comfortably far off. She wasn't staying. She would not have time to become so enmeshed in his life.

He stepped from the shower, grabbed a towel and paused. They had no future. Maybe he needed to stop wasting his time getting all worked up. If he went into this knowing it had a short shelf-life, maybe they both could enjoy themselves. If she was willing. If she was as interested in him as she seemed to be, maybe they could enjoy a few days or weeks together. Afterward, she'd be out of his life forever.

～

After her shower, Caitlin dressed and limped back to the kitchen to re-bandage her foot herself, then sweep up any sand they'd left behind.

Mrs. Smith came in as she pulled on thick socks.

"Good heavens, what happened to you? Are you all right?" She set some shopping bags on the counter and turned to Caitlin, hands-on-hips, and surveyed the remains of her first aid— the open kit, gauze and a tape dispenser on the table.

"A little damage control. I stepped on something on the beach. Sorry for any mess we made. I'll sweep up."

Mrs. Smith ignored her offer. "You were out there, barefoot?"

"Aye, well, Holt and I had a wee contest to see which was colder, the ocean or a loch. So I had to take off my shoes."

Mrs. Smith laughed at that. "And who won?"

"Actually, we never came to a decision. A wave knocked me under, and Holt had to rescue me." A warm tingle ran down her spine at the memory of being held in Holt's arms. Caitlin wanted to wallow in the feeling, but with Mrs. Smith eyeing her, she pushed it away, finished replacing supplies in the kit and closed it.

Mrs. Smith gave her a speculative look. "As long as you're sure you don't need stitches." When Caitlin shook her head, she turned back to her groceries.

"'Tisn't bad," she managed to say. "I'll get out of your way soon." As she put the kit in the drawer where Holt had found it, her gaze fell on the picture on the window ledge. "I don't want to pry, but that's a fine-looking lad. Who is he?"

Mrs. Smith paused from putting away groceries to smile at the photo. "My son, on the day he graduated from basic training. He lived here while he went to school, then joined the service."

"He's very handsome." What was it about men in uniform? It seemed to make a square jaw sharper, the glint in the eye more steely.

"Thank you." Mrs. Smith gazed at the picture for a moment longer, then seemed to recollect herself. "Dinner will be ready in an hour, dear. You should go upstairs and rest until then"

"Brilliant. I'll take your advice."

An hour later, Caitlin limped a bit on the way down to dinner. The gash in her foot hurt like mad if she put too much weight on it but was not enough to require a doctor.

Holt glanced at her foot as she walked in the small dining room. She forced herself not to limp, despite the discomfort it caused.

He didn't mention her injury or ask why she hadn't let him re-bandage it. Nor did he mention their contest or anything that followed. She tamped down on the disappointment that hollowed out her chest. True, he'd been rescuing her, but the touching and the heated looks, she hadn't imagined them, right? Instead, now he behaved as if they hadn't been wrapped in each other's arms a few hours earlier. He'd retreated back into himself, and for the entire dinner, didn't have much more to say than politeness required.

When the dessert course arrived, Holt announced casually, "I need to run into town tomorrow morning. Is there anything I can pick up for you while I'm there?"

Caitlin knew an opportunity when she saw one and wasn't going to let this one pass her by. Going with Holt would save her a drive on the wrong side of the road, and might give her a chance, away from the estate he loathed, to see him unbend even more than he had in the water today. In any case, she could deliver the coffee she'd promised Doc Coates, then if there was time, do some quick shopping for gifts for Farrell and Mrs. Smith.

"Actually, I owe a visit to a…friend…before the holiday." What did one call one's rescuers? Not a friend exactly, but acquaintance didn't feel right, either, not for Holt and not for Doc Coates. "Perhaps I could do that while you're busy, then you could pick me up?" She could see the wheels turning in Holt's mind as he debated how much of an imposition her request would be on his time and plans. After much less cogitation than was his usual practice, he nodded.

"Sure. No problem. Will you be okay walking on your cut foot?"

Finally! So he did remember what happened today. Caitlin appreciated his concern, no matter how belatedly he expressed it. "I'll be fine."

He studied her for a moment, then asked, "Can you be ready to leave right after breakfast?"

Did he doubt her word? If she didn't want him to do her this favor, she might have challenged him on that look, but she didn't want him to withdraw his offer. "Aye," she said, sipping her wine. "Earlier, if you need…"

"After breakfast will work," Holt said around his last bite of cake. He rose and headed for the door, then turned back. "Wear something warm. It's supposed to snow tomorrow."

"Thanks, I will." She grimaced at his retreating back. Though they'd discussed where she came from several times, including during their contest on the beach, he still didn't seem to understand that she came from a cold climate in Scotland, and she was perfectly capable of taking care of herself.

CHAPTER 5

The next morning, Caitlin made sure her cut heel was bandaged and padded enough to let her walk comfortably, then got some work done before she heard Holt come down for his breakfast. She had another cup of tea while he ate, then went to grab her coat. She arrived in the foyer in time to see Holt pull the estate's Mercedes SUV up to the front portico. So he trusted her to be on time. Or perhaps, he simply intended to warm the car so their drive would be more comfortable. He did have a considerate side, even if, like his smile, he rarely chose to display it.

She wrapped her scarf around her neck and stepped outside. The sudden cold took her breath for a moment. "Hiya. You were right," she announced as she slid into her seat, intending to reward his consideration with an appeal to his male ego. "It's much colder than yesterday. I hope whatever you have planned in the village is indoors."

Holt kept his gaze averted as he pulled from the drive

onto the street. "Business is typically conducted in an office, so yes, indoors. What about you? Where shall I drop you?"

"Do you know where Dr. Coates's office is?"

Holt's gaze cut to her. "Doctor? Is your foot infected? Are you ill?"

She appreciated his show of concern but sighed in relief when he turned his attention back to the road in front of them. "Nay, no' even a wee. Dr. Coates is a veterinarian. A friend." She'd never told Holt about the attempted purse-snatching but now was as good a time as any. "He saved me from getting nicked my first trip to the village. I think you call it a mugging."

"You were mugged?" Holt's gaze left the road again. This time, he frowned at her. "You never told me. That bandage on your hand yesterday…?"

She lifted her hand and displayed a thin, pink line, all that remained of her injury. "A scratch from the buckle on my purse strap. I refused to let go of it. Thanks to Dr. Coates, there was little to tell." She shrugged as Holt returned his attention to the road.

"Then tell me the little there is," he said. A muscle in his jaw flexed. Was he angry? That she hadn't told him? Or about what happened to her?

"A man…a lad, really…tried to nick my purse. Dr. Coates was nearby and heard me yelling. He grabbed the thief, got my purse back, and held the lad until the local constable arrived and took charge of him."

"I'm…sorry. And embarrassed you had such an unfortunate introduction to the village."

Since when did he care what anyone thought about anything in this area? He was fighting to leave as quickly as he could, wasn't he? "Ach, nay. Actually, it was quite fortunate. Otherwise, I might never have met the doctor or Alice Nash, the lady who owns the bakery."

Holt frowned again. "Sounds like he did a good job rescuing you."

Was he equating that with yesterday's adventure in the sound? "Are you saying I need a lot of rescuing? Or that you think I'm unlucky? Getting mugged wasn't my fault."

"Of course not. You're lucky the vet heard you."

"Aye, he was very nice," she answered, somewhat mollified. "According to Alice, he's been in the village only two years. He's done so much in that time. A successful veterinary practice, in the Army before that. He trains service dogs, too."

"Admirable."

Did Holt's jaw look a wee more tense? Surely he wasn't jealous. He'd never met the man, and she'd given no indication Doc Coates was more than a friend. Surprised, she changed the subject and spent the next few minutes directing Holt to the veterinary practice. Once Holt stopped the car in front of it, she reached for the door handle. "How long do you think your business will take?"

"No more than an hour and a half," Holt responded, his gaze on the building.

Caitlin glanced around. One of the vet techs was walking a medium-sized dog with a missing front leg. She glanced back in time to see Holt wince. In sympathy for the dog? He might be an ultra-rich captain of the dot-com industry, but there was a heart in there somewhere. One he kept well-hidden and took out only to rescue damsels in distress. And maybe animals, too. "When you're done, just come in and ask the receptionist, Rachel. She'll ken where I am. Um…you're not allergic to dogs or cats, are you?"

"Not that I'm aware." His gaze followed the three-legged dog as the tech led it around the side of the building, then Holt's brow furrowed. He sighed when it disappeared.

If he'd had a pet, he'd know if he was allergic. How sad. Caitlin took pity on him and didn't remark on his reaction to the dog, but his sympathy for it reassured her.

"Great. I'll see you in an hour or so." She opened the door and popped out before he could respond. As soon as she closed it, he pulled away. Caitlin stood on the sidewalk, watching as his brake lights came on and he rounded the next corner. Caitlin suspected Holt had depths he'd yet to reveal, but she liked the hints she'd gotten from him yesterday and today.

~

*H*olt met with Mr. Thornton, the lawyer who had shown up in his California office. After reading through the papers Thornton left on Holt's desk that day, Holt had a few procedural questions, but the one item forefront in his mind was the paper he'd found from his alma mater.

"You are correct," Thornton told him, to Holt's disbelief. "Your great-aunt funded the scholarship that allowed you to attend Stanford."

"Why would she have done that?" Holt demanded, though he suspected he knew the reason. Sending him to school across the country had been another way to punish his mother.

"Her reasons were never communicated to me," Thornton told him. "But her gift served to provide you with an excellent education and gave you the start to the successful life you've made for yourself."

Holt didn't see anything to be gained by arguing the point with him. If Thornton wanted to think the best of Holt's great-aunt, he wouldn't waste time trying to dissuade him.

"Do you intend to remain for the stipulated period to retain the estate?"

Now that he had seen the property, he was no less eager to unload it than he had been in California when he got the news about his inheritance. "Besides being dragged into court, what happens if I refuse the bequest?"

"It becomes the property of the local jurisdiction. I understand some developers are already filing paperwork to buy it. They would change the character of the area forever, I fear."

Holt could imagine what Caitlin's reaction would be to some local politician disposing of the estate. And of a developer tearing down the house to build something else. Condos? Even he couldn't stomach the idea. She'd be furious, but even though he was beginning to see some of what she appreciated in the estate, he had not changed his mind about getting rid of it. Thornton's comment only cemented Holt's resolve that he would be the one to determine what happened to it. "At my office, you mentioned that brief visits away are allowed."

"As long as you clear them with me."

"Our meeting today is well-timed, then. I have a contracts meeting in New York City starting tomorrow. I'll take the train and return as soon as my business is finished. Likely no more than three days."

Thornton agreed, of course. Holt knew he would. It was a necessary and reasonable business-related request.

His next meeting, with a real estate attorney, would tell him more about putting the estate on the market. He killed some time before the appointment, walking around the village. Every shop window he passed boasted a riot of red and green ribbons, evergreen boughs, wrapped presents, or fake snow and crystals suspended from the ceiling on nearly invisible fishing line. The colors and sparkles caught his gaze, but images of Caitlin with this Doctor Coates, the veterinarian, kept intruding.

The cold water yesterday and the Christmas decorations in the village today must have frozen his brain's logic centers. That could be the only explanation for why he stood here longing for some fantasy full of colored lights, unwrapping presents— or undressing Caitlin— and happy endings.

It was too soon after the Helen debacle to take up with another woman, especially one he'd known for only two, no, three days. He had to stop thinking about Caitlin that way, but it didn't stop him from wondering what kind of friend the doc was to her. Her enthusiasm, as she'd told him about the vet and his good works, made Holt's blood pressure rise. In addition to apparently having a heart of gold, was he tall and handsome? No woman in her prime could resist that combination.

Caitlin was definitely a woman in her prime with curves in all the right places that felt like heaven in his arms. Her smile ranged from sweet to snarky, and she had a temperament to match. Intelligent. Dedicated, with a sterling reputation in her profession. If he had any sense, he'd go after her. Since their visit to the beach, the thought of her with another man made his jaw lock.

Was he jealous? And of someone he'd never met? Ridiculous. Impossible. He shouldn't care. Before long, he would return to California, and she to Scotland. But the idea persisted.

After the meeting with the realtor, he reclaimed his car, then parked on the street in front of the vet's office and took a breath. He saw only one way to put his wild imaginings to rest. Meet the man. Watch Caitlin interact with him. Accept whatever he observed and get on with his life back in California as quickly as possible.

A bell tinkled over the door as he entered. Tiny twinkling white lights framed the interior of every window. Construction paper ornaments shaped like dog biscuits, and kittens and puppies with wings were strung across the glass and embellished with names spelled out in glitter. Holt surmised they must be the names of peoples' pets. Silver garland and shiny red and green balls draped the front of the reception desk. A small, decorated tree sat on a corner table. Holiday music played low in the background, almost covered by the occasional outraged feline yowl or canine whine. A whiff of animal urine and wet fur made him wrinkle his nose. A few people sat with animal carriers on their laps or larger dogs at their feet, the dogs' tails thumping in excitement— or more likely, anxiety. He sympathized.

"I'm looking for Caitlin Paterson," he told the girl at the desk. "I'm supposed to meet her here."

"You must be Mr. Ridley," the girl answered with a blazing white smile. "It's nice to meet you. I'm Rachel. Merry Christmas."

"Um…Merry Christmas." He summoned a smile.

The girl nodded. "Follow me." She gestured to an adjoining hallway.

Holt followed her down a long hall lined with examination rooms. If Caitlin was alone with the vet in his office, Holt hoped he wouldn't walk in on anything too friendly.

"Here we are," the receptionist announced cheerily. "Caitlin, your friend Mr. Ridley is here."

The receptionist moved out of the way, and Holt found himself looking into another exam room. Caitlin was stripping off gloves as she turned toward him. The vet, if that is who he was, was putting a puppy into a carrier, his back to Holt. The lab coat hid his build, but he appeared to be a little shorter than Holt.

"Thanks, Rachel. Holt Ridley," Caitlin said as she walked forward, then took Holt's arm. "Come meet Doc Coates."

The vet turned around and pulled off his gloves, then

held out a hand to Holt. "I'm pleased to meet you, Mr. Ridley. Caitlin has had a lot of nice things to say about you."

Caitlin had nice things to say about him? Since when? "Good to meet you, too." Holt shook his hand while he studied the man. He was older than Holt had imagined, with a little silver sprinkled in his hair, but his build was still trim and strong, as was his grip. He looked familiar, yet Holt was sure they'd never met. The vet seemed to consider him, too. Holt nearly asked, but Caitlin interrupted.

"I've told Holt what little I know about what you do here, Doc, but if you have a few minutes, I hoped you might show him more."

"I don't want to take up your time," Holt objected, thinking of the crowded waiting room. "I'm sure you're busy."

"Not at the moment. My techs are dealing with the routine cases— vaccinations and so forth. This little guy," he said, gesturing at the puppy in the carrier, "just finished his wellness check. He's going to board with us while his foster family is out of town for the holidays. He's also one of the potential search-and-rescue trainees."

Caitlin beamed at the puppy, then at the vet.

Holt fought to keep a frown from his face. "That's very interes—"

"Doc Coates," the receptionist called as she burst into the room, cheeks red against her suddenly pale face. "Someone just brought in a puppy that might have Parvo."

"Put them in the nearest empty exam room. I'll be right

there." He turned to include both Caitlin and Holt in his gaze. "I'm sorry, but this is dangerous for the other canine patients. I've got to go." He gave Holt a quick nod. "Thanks for stopping by."

"I still owe you a coffee," Caitlin told him as he left, not quite at a run.

Holt heard him exchange a few words with his receptionist, then the hallway got quiet again, except for a faint Christmas melody that suddenly seemed out of place.

"I hope that puppy is all right," Caitlin said, her gaze on the door. Then the puppy in the room with them whined, and Caitlin stepped over to its carrier. "Don't ye *fash*, ye wee lad. Ye'll be fine. They'll take good care of ye here."

"We'd better go," Holt said, suddenly eager to get away from this place. Caitlin's interaction with the vet had been too brief for Holt to determine anything about their relationship, but at any rate, she seemed to be getting way too attached to the puppy. He couldn't argue with its cuteness, but he did not need her to decide that fostering it over the holidays would make their Christmas complete.

∼

*A*fter they left the veterinary office, Holt remained quiet, his gaze on the traffic that had appeared since their trip into town.

In moments, the silence became heavy, weighted with Caitlin's own disappointment that he hadn't had more time to learn about the search and rescue work Doc Coates told her about. To break it, she asked, "Last-minute shoppers?"

Holt glanced at her, then back at the road. "What?"

"All the cars, all of a sudden. I'm wondering if they're all last-minute shoppers. Christmas is coming, ye ken."

"Oh. Maybe."

"No, really. Christmas is coming," she replied and waited for a reaction to her jest.

Holt glanced aside at her, then back at the road.

Disappointed that stone-faced Holt was back, she cast about for something to say. "Of course," she added after checking the analog clock on the dashboard, "it is nearly lunchtime. Everyone could be on the way to their favorite takeaway."

"Takeaway?"

"Um, where ye pick up food and take it back to the office."

"Take-out. Or carry-out," he said with more animation. "Or a fast food place. Burgers, pizza, fried chicken." Holt glanced at her then back at the road.

He seemed more relaxed now that they were away from the vet's office. She liked it when he became more open, more talkative, and wanted him to stay that way. "Another thing that's simpler in Scotland," she told him. "Takeaway. Done. Usually Indian, or fish and chips."

"Are you hungry?"

"I wasn't, but then I mentioned fish and chips— not that I expect you'll have anything like good Scottish fish and chips here."

Holt quirked an eyebrow. "You might be surprised. Mrs. Smith suggested a seafood place with the best lobster rolls on the island. Fish and chips, too, I'll bet."

"Really?" Caitlin's stomach growled.

"There's my answer." Holt turned at the next cross street and headed out of town, at right angles to the road back to the estate. "Don't worry, it's just far enough to let your appetite develop."

"Who are you and what have you done with Holt Ridley?" Caitlin muttered under her breath, happy to see him unwind.

In moments, the village gave way to forest-lined streets, then to a wider, faster highway, and the trees changed from the mix of hardwoods and pines in the area surrounding the village and the estate to short pines. In the suddenly sandy-looking soil, the trees grew sparse and spindly. Caitlin got glimpses of water through breaks in the trees. "There's nothing out here. Are you sure you know where you're going?"

"Have a little faith," Holt replied, a quirk on his full lips.

Caitlin eyed him in disbelief. He'd almost smiled. She could get used to seeing him smile. And laugh, she thought, recalling the day she'd cut her foot. For the most part, those expressions had been un-Holt-like. Maybe this meant he was warming to her. Heartened, she turned back to take in the view, which was becoming more and more beachy. Suddenly buildings appeared, and after a few whizzed by, Holt slowed and turned the car into a car park. Until he stopped the car, the tires crunched on the white shell fragments that covered the sandy ground.

"Watch your step," Holt advised as he got out. "Let me know if your foot hurts."

Caitlin exited the car to tinny Christmas music from

the restaurant's outdoor speakers. She took a few tentative steps, feeling the shells shift beneath her feet.

Holt came around the bonnet and put a hand on the small of her back.

Was he going to pull her into his arms and carry her to the door?

"The oyster shells rock a bit if they're not dug into the sand, but you'll get the hang of it." He turned her and walked beside her toward the building.

"Everyone does, it seems," Caitlin remarked, glancing around at the nearly full car park to avoid looking at Holt. She kicked herself for sounding whiney instead of droll, but she deserved congratulations for being capable of speech. Her face had to be red in response to the heat radiating from Holt's hand on her back. She hadn't expected his touch, but even less, her immediate, overpowering reaction to it— her desire for him to take her in his arms. She'd nearly turned into him and burrowed into his embrace like a child. That rescue on the beach made her sensitive to his touch. She wanted more. A bad idea, that. And not just because the car park was dotted here and there with people coming and going. Holt was too near, too warm, and his grip was too firm as he encouraged her toward their destination. It reinforced the impression his trim, but muscular physique had given her when they first met, even more so as he carried her to the house from the beach and moved around the kitchen with wet clothes sticking to his body. His hand on her lower back now made her even more curious about what delights he kept hidden under that buttoned-up exterior.

"You're doing fine," Holt encouraged her after a minute, releasing her to open a screen door and gesture her through.

He had no idea. Fine didn't begin to describe what she was feeling. Other than being glad to be back on a smooth surface, even if it was only stained concrete, Caitlin regretted Holt no longer needed to steady her. Or so she thought. His touch had done something to her equilibrium. Or maybe it was just low blood sugar. While Holt arranged for a table with the lass at the reception desk, Caitlin took deep breaths to restore herself. Mouthwatering scents filled her nose.

Before her stomach could growl loudly enough to embarrass her, Holt beckoned for her to follow the hostess to their table, then handed her into her seat. The hostess left them each a lengthy menu and the promise that their server would be right with them.

"Lobster rolls, ye say? I've never heard of them," Caitlin said as they picked up their menus. She glanced down its contents until she spotted what she wanted.

Holt nodded. "You might have if you hadn't locked yourself in the midst of dusty old— very old— furnishings for days. The only breaks you've taken have been to go into the village, where you got mugged. And again with me."

"Checked up on me, have ye?"

"Farrell filled me in on what you've been doing, though he neglected to mention the mugging. And I have been there for part of the time since you arrived."

"Aye, well, some of those old— and some ancient— furnishings are quite interesting to me. And valuable."

"Not all of them?"

"Nay." Caitlin set her menu aside. She didn't need it to order what she hoped were the best fish and chips on the island. "The precious pieces are where you might expect—where visitors to the house see them. The more private spaces tend to have more disposable furnishings which, I expect, have changed over time with fashions and the family's taste."

"Makes sense. So—"

Their server interrupted at that point and took their orders.

"So?" Caitlin prompted once they were alone again.

"How much more do you have to do?"

"I've done a cursory look in the bedrooms and the upstairs parlor but want to get a closer look at a few pieces up there." Warming to her favorite subject, she went on to describe the ones that had caught her eye but cut short her explanation when she saw Holt's gaze wandering around the room. His attention clearly had wandered, too. She clamped down on her irritation. She'd hoped her enthusiasm for the estate and its contents would begin to sway Holt in its favor, but she'd been fooling herself. "As for the main floor, I'm nearly done." Caitlin frowned at the thought. She should be glad to finish a job where she was so at odds with the client's wishes. It would allow her to return home for the holidays rather than remain here with strangers, but for some reason, she wasn't eager to leave.

"Is there a problem?"

Damn, Holt noticed her frown. She needed to guard her expression more carefully. "Nay. I was just trying to recall how many days until Christmas. I don't mind missing it so much, but I would like to be home for Hogmanay— New Year's to ye."

Holt frowned at that. "So, you'll be here for an American Christmas. Of course, you're welcome at the estate, though you won't find much of the spirit of the season there."

Caitlin nodded. "I know you said you wanted me to finish quickly, but I don't think I can do a proper job and be gone before Yule. Christmas."

"No. I...that's fine. You should know I'm going to the city for work tomorrow. I'll be back in a few days. But that makes me think. If you wanted to see an American Christmas, New York City is a good place to experience it all."

"Are you asking me to go with you?"

He leaned back, his expression suddenly hooded. "No, not this time."

"Is there a problem?" Caitlin echoed his earlier question.

"I will be in meetings the entire time I'm there. And you said you have more to do. You did say you wanted to be home for New Years."

"Okay." Caitlin chided herself for thinking he would offer to show her the city. But her stomach sank at the thought of days without having the distraction of Holt around to talk to. To spar with. "I thought the will said you had to remain at the estate." On the other hand, with him out of the way, she'd get a lot more work done.

"And here you go," a waiter interrupted before Holt could answer, setting beers and baskets of fried fish and chips for her and a lobster roll for him in front of them. "Is there anything else you need?"

A thick wedge of lemon decorated one side of the pile of golden-brown breaded and fried fish, and Caitlin had noticed the bottle of malt vinegar on the table earlier, so she shook her head.

"We're fine," Holt told him.

"Thanks," Caitlin added. Despite wondering what else Holt had been about to say, she turned her attention to lunch. After a few bites, she told Holt, "You were right. This is good. Not quite up to Scottish standards," she added with a grin, "but entirely acceptable." She broke off a piece of the fried fish and handed it to him. "Taste that."

He chewed for a moment, swallowed, and said, "If the Scots have something better than this, I want to taste it. I'll have to come over so you can show me all your favorite spots."

Caitlin nodded, butterflies suddenly fluttering among the bites of fish in her belly. Her favorite spots? She could take that several ways, at least one having nothing to do with food, but everything to do with enjoyment. She studied him while he focused on his food. Had he meant the double entendre, or was she reading more into his comment than she should? At the very least, for a change, Holt only seemed to be trying to charm her. Would he really come to Scotland? Surely not just to try the fish and chips. For her? She sipped her beer, trying to cool the fire that bloomed in her blood. "I have a few ye would enjoy," she allowed. "But it's a long flight from California."

"My business does take me to Europe now and again. I could show up on your doorstep someday."

An image filled her mind of Holt at her door, stepping inside, and then pulling her into his arms. *Ach*, she had to stop that right there. Heat was climbing her neck, and she knew her face was going to be red in moments. "Ye're welcome any time," she managed to say, grabbed a chip and dribbled enough malt vinegar on it to clear her sinuses for a week— or explain her sudden excess color.

~

Holt took a bite of his lobster roll, trying to distract himself from the blush staining Caitlin's cheeks. So she'd realized, just as he had, that his earlier statement could be taken several ways, as could her response.

He'd like to explore her favorite spots, the ones that had nothing to do with food. Or sightseeing. Only with her. He dropped his gaze to his basket to keep Caitlin from seeing the desire for her in his eyes. He had no business letting such thoughts overtake him. Better he kept his gaze and his thoughts on the heaped fries and the soft roll bursting with lobster meat. He was about to be gone for three days, and after that? He might be stuck here through the winter, but she wasn't.

Still, he could see himself arriving in Scotland at her door, which made him wonder. Did she live in a house? An apartment, or flat, if they used that term in Scotland and not just in England? Would there be a roommate in the way? If so, he would let Caitlin take him to her favorite spots of a different kind. While showing him around her country, they would find the privacy he imagined they would want.

He wasn't sure what their relationship was at the moment. Boss and employee? Contractor and client? Friends? Potential lovers? Going to Scotland to see Caitlin could lead to more than either of them were prepared for at this moment. The hell with playing tourist. He could easily imagine what would happen between them, at least up to a point. It bothered him that he didn't know what it would mean to either of them. At the end, he would leave, and she would remain. Was it worth the pain of that leave-taking? Or of reinventing a relationship neither was certain of while they were here? When she left for home, she might forget all about him. He might meet someone and forget all about her. He could be wasting his time enjoying any sort of future encounter with her. He should let this drop before he said or did something monumentally stupid.

So why couldn't he?

She certainly recognized the double entendre she'd used, whether she did it intentionally or not. Her color had climbed quickly soon after she spoke, giving her skin a rosy hue that made him imagine that heat spreading to other parts of her body. And making him hard.

Using the vinegar to try to disguise her reaction was clever, but an act of desperation to hide the desire her blush gave away. Or was it embarrassment? That thought sent a cold wash of disappointment through him. Perhaps she wasn't as into him as he'd been convincing himself with his daydreams. They might be a foolish waste of time, but if he was right, there was something going on between them. No, they weren't foolish. He was right.

He hid a smirk, amused at himself, but also intrigued and getting more and more interested in her, despite what his head and his recent experience with another woman were telling him. Something was developing between them. Something that might be worth exploring, if only they had the time. He made a mental note to have his office look into her background, surprised he didn't think of it before. The lawyer could give him whatever bona fides his firm used to decide to hire her, but Holt's interest went well beyond that. Whether it should or not.

He hated the necessity, but he'd learned he needed to be more careful than he had in the past. No matter how much Caitlin Paterson intrigued him, he would take whatever this was slowly. His upcoming trip to the city was well-timed. Their adventure on the beach had brought them closer very quickly. His desire for her had spiked while he held her up in the rough surf. He had felt her heart pounding in her chest and watched it pulse in the vein in her throat. And carrying her to the house had made it clear to him that she felt the pull, too. There was no question that both of them were interested in the other. But one important question remained— should they be?

CHAPTER 6

After his trip to the city, Holt was impatient to hear what progress Caitlin had made during the days he'd been gone. He told himself that was all he was eager for, but in truth, he'd missed her. He'd been busy, but that hadn't stopped him from thinking of her when he spotted an auburn-haired woman on the sidewalk ahead of him. Even a bit of overheard conversation in an accent like hers at a coffee shop could make him look for her, then feel like a fool.

For a change, he came downstairs to find Caitlin hadn't yet made an appearance. They both must be getting over the jet lag from their respective time zones. "Good morning," he greeted Mrs. Smith. "Just some coffee and toast will do for me," he told her.

"Nonsense," she replied, reaching for a skillet. "Bacon and eggs, at least. You won't get far on toast."

He gave in and settled back with his coffee while she made his breakfast. "No sign of Caitlin yet?"

"No," she told him as she slid eggs next to the bacon on his plate. "She must be sleeping in." Mrs. Smith set toast, butter, and jam in front of him while he dug into his breakfast, then puttered about, putting the kitchen to rights. "What do you have planned for today?"

"Nothing this early," he told her. "California isn't awake yet."

"Have you looked up anyone you used to know since you've been back? Friends from school? Neighbors?"

"No, not yet." Given that his initial plan had been to do a quick survey and leave as soon as possible, Holt hadn't considered going back to any of his old haunts. But once the idea took root, he decided even if he didn't contact anyone he used to know, today was as good a day as any to spend some more time away from the estate. After devoting an intense three days in meetings in the city, taking a break from his business might do him some good. He considered waiting for Caitlin to see if she wanted to go with him, but after he thought about it, Holt realized he didn't know what he'd find, or how he'd react to being in his old neighborhood. He decided it would be better to go without her. He'd talk to her when he got back to the estate.

He finished eating and thanked Mrs. Smith. Then he gathered his jacket, gloves, and hat and headed to the garage, jangling a set of keys in his hand as he walked from bay to bay to the vehicle he wanted. Not the Mercedes SUV this time. Something less noticeable, less ostentatious. A jeep with a few years on it caught his eye. Perfect.

His memories of this end of Long Island were far from

fond. But he found Caitlin's enthusiasm and his lawyer's revelation that his great-aunt paid his college bills were starting to open him to the possibility that his recollections were skewed by the bitterness he'd inherited from his mother. He'd have a look around and see if things were different enough to put old resentments in the past, where they belonged. There was so much about his mother's history— and his own— he didn't know. Perhaps Caitlin was right, and it was time for him to start finding out.

He headed west and south toward the village where he and his mother lived until he went away to college on an academic scholarship— one he believed he'd won through diligent study and the ethos of hard work he'd learned from her. Until his meeting with Thornton, who told him the truth, he'd never known otherwise. He'd jumped to the conclusion that his great-aunt had sent him as far from his mother as she could, but perhaps her motive had been more benign, or even more altruistic, wanting to ease her guilt, and to ensure that he could escape the life he'd lived with his mother. It was a novel idea, and one he wasn't sure he believed in, but it was a crack in the hard shell of bitterness he'd built up all his life. His great-aunt was actually behind the scholarship, and Holt could either let that news eat at him until the day he died or take advantage of his time in the area to learn as much as he could.

Their old neighborhood wasn't far from the estate, but it could have been another world. He shouldn't have been surprised by how much the village had changed since he'd moved. But he'd always thought the south fork of Long Island had a timeless quality, so the differences surprised him. More traffic, more strip shopping centers, more apartments, balconies draped with colored lights and the occasional wreath to mark the season. To him, this area had always suffered by contrast with the area around the estate, but over the years the contrast had sharpened. If this was the alternative, no wonder Caitlin wanted to preserve what he had at the estate.

He turned onto the street where he and his mother had lived. After driving for several blocks, he began to think his memory was faulty. The tree-lined streets, the little house, in fact, the entire area, was gone, replaced by more apartments and parking lots, with not a soul in sight. The transformation saddened him. Their little neighborhood hadn't been much, but now that he was here, he recalled a sense of community, kids playing outside until dark, riding bikes in the shade of grand old trees in the summer, neighbors who knew and looked out for each other's kids.

He made a few turns and found the small office building where his mother, who had always been good with math, had done bookkeeping for several local businesses. The accounting firm's name was missing from the sign outside. Another link to his past gone.

He turned the car back toward the estate, passing the library where she'd worked part-time so he could check out unlimited amounts of books. They'd both been voracious readers, and it had been one of the few places he felt he belonged— back then. Seeing it changed inside— that last vestige of a love he shared with his mother— would hurt too much. He didn't stop.

Instead, he drove a few blocks farther and pulled into

Charlie's, his favorite hang-out when he'd been in high school. If the family still owned the business, maybe he could ask some questions. Charlie's son, Jack, had been a classmate.

"Look what the cat dragged in!" Jack's voice was unmistakable, even after more than a decade, as was the grin he directed Holt's way from behind the counter. "I'd know you anywhere, Holt Ridley."

Holt held out a hand. "Jack Romano. Good to see you." Jack looked heavier, a bit more lined, but other than that, much the same. They'd played on the school lacrosse team together.

"Damn, it's been, what, nearly fifteen years?"

"Since graduation, yes."

He gestured to an empty booth by the front window. "Sit. What are you having? The lunch rush hasn't started yet. I'll join you."

"One with everything, of course."

"Beer?"

"No, a half-and-half, I think." The fifty/fifty mix of iced tea and lemonade, a local favorite, was known as an Arnold Palmer everywhere but in this area. "I've got a lot of ground to cover today."

"Be right with you." He pushed through a swinging door at the end of the counter, yelling, "Anita!"

Holt let himself relax in the familiar surroundings. Same Formica tabletops, same red pleather bench seats in the booths. Some might have been reupholstered, but if so, care had been taken to make sure they matched. He smiled and inhaled scents of tomato sauce, pizza spices, and toasted cheese with an overtone of spilled beer. At least one place in his past hadn't changed.

After a few minutes, Jack returned with Holt's drink, two small white plates, and a beer for himself. "Anita will bring the pie when it's ready. You remember Anita Russo? In the class behind ours? She's a Romano now. I married her."

Holt nodded, picturing a petite girl with lustrous, dark hair. "How long ago?"

"Ten years and three kids." Jack shook his head. "Best years of my life, so far." He lifted his glass in a mock toast and took a drink.

"No kidding? With three kids?"

"Sure. They're a pain, but they're also a lot of fun. Gotta have someone to leave this place to someday like my old man did to me. You married?"

"No." Holt's stomach sank. The way he let work consume him, he never would be married, especially if all the women he met were like Helen Conroe. Not that Caitlin was anything like her. But even Caitlin would be out of reach once she returned to Scotland. He'd always heard long-distance relationships were difficult and complicated. The distance between California and Scotland would make theirs impossible. Holt chewed on that for a moment. He hadn't been thinking in terms of a relationship with Caitlin Paterson, at least not one that involved more than some fun while they were both here. But the idea of Scotland being so far away that he would never see her again didn't sit well with him.

Anita arrived with the pizza before he could try to

analyze the empty feeling in his gut. The tantalizing scent of sauce, meats, and veggies distracted him into thinking he must just be hungry.

Anita was a slightly rounder, softer version of the girl Holt remembered, with a few silver strands showing in her dark hair, now cut short. He stood to greet her.

"Holt! It's great to see you." She put the pizza on the table and stepped closer to her husband.

"You look as gorgeous as ever, Mrs. Romano," Holt told her, saddened that he hadn't known her well enough to get a hug or, at least, a hand on his arm that a friend might have offered.

"Hey!" Jack teased. "That's *my* girl." He tucked an arm around her waist, and she leaned down for a kiss.

"It's great to see you two so happy." Holt smiled to hide the twinge of envy coursing through him.

"We're doing all right," Anita said with a smile. "I'll leave you two to catch up." She returned to the kitchen.

Holt resumed his seat. After they'd both had a bite of excellent pizza, Holt asked Jack, "How is your dad?"

Jack grinned. "Enjoying his retirement in Florida, lucky bastard." He sobered. "I'm sorry about your mother. It's been, what, five years?"

"Six."

"She used to come in here now and again with some friends." He paused, then asked, "So what brings you back?"

Holt sipped his drink before answering. "Her aunt left me her beach cottage. I'm wandering down memory lane while I decide what to do with it."

"Wow, must be worth a fortune. A lot of upkeep, huh?"

"You could say that." He snagged another slice of pizza. "And since I've been away, I've lost track of everyone. Do you know if any of those friends of my mother's are still in the area?"

Jack shook his head. "Sorry, not a clue. Haven't seen any of them in years."

So the ones she came here with might have been co-workers at the defunct accounting firm, not friends. Holt pulled out one of his cards and wrote his private number on the back. "If you see any of them, could you ask them to give me a call? I have some family history questions. People she knew might have some answers."

Jack took it and tucked it in a pocket. "Sure. Be happy to."

They finished the pizza, and after telling Anita goodbye and getting a brotherly pounding on the back from Jack, Holt left. He hadn't found any answers, but reconnecting with old friends had felt good. Better than he'd expected. He wondered what Caitlin would think about where he'd been. She'd probably tease him for unbending enough to find anything from his past he could enjoy. The idea of that felt good, too.

~

When Caitlin came down for a late breakfast — or early lunch— she was surprised to find out that Holt got up early and had gone out. "He's not still asleep?" She had worked late last night doing research online while waiting for Holt to return from the city. Once she heard him come in and go straight to his room, she finally was able to shut down her laptop and go to sleep.

"I believe he decided to look up some former acquaintances," Mrs. Smith told her as she set a sandwich in front of her.

Caitlin dropped into a chair at the kitchen table. Really? She didn't know what to say to that. Holt hadn't shown any interest in any part of his past not involved in unloading this estate. She barely noticed what she was eating as she took a bite and chewed, thoughtfully. "What made him decide to do that, I wonder."

"I asked if he'd looked up any old classmates and such," Mrs. Smith admitted. "He seemed taken with the idea, and off he went."

Caitlin nodded. This development might be very good. If he reconnected with old friends and his walk down memory lane showed him that things were better here than he remembered, he might finally see a reason to keep the estate.

Farrell came into the kitchen then. "If you're looking for Mr. Ridley, he drove away hours ago."

"We know," Caitlin and Mrs. Smith replied together, then they chuckled.

"I wonder if he'll change his mind about decorating the house," Mrs. Smith said. "Farrell, the decorations are all up in the attic—"

"Attic?" Caitlin broke in. "How did I not know ye had things stored in an attic?"

"Most people do around here," Farrell said.

Caitlin kicked herself. Ye daft *eedjit*, of course, there was an attic in this pile. "What's in it, besides Christmas decorations?"

"Why, a lot of old things," Mrs. Smith answered. "I thought you knew…"

Her job might have just gotten much more complicated. Caitlin shook her head. "How do I get up there?"

"Farrell, will you do the honors? After both of you finish eating?"

"Of course," he replied. Once the meal was over, and Mrs. Smith allowed them to leave, he led Caitlin to a set of stairs that had been hidden by what she assumed was a closet door in an empty, unused bedroom.

"Give a shout if you need anything," Farrell told her and went on about his business.

Caitlin mounted the stairs, determined not to let her hopes get the best of her. Still, attics were often treasure troves. Perhaps this attic would be full of the very sort of things she'd come here to find. Not high-quality English or Scottish antiques of the first water, the kind on display in the parlor downstairs, but pieces reminiscent of Scottish history. Perhaps even Jacobite pieces carted off by murderous and avaricious English lords who took control of much of Scotland after Culloden, then brought their spoils to the colonies sometime later.

Or there might be nothing of value. Junk that no one had the heart to discard. Broken pieces of an earlier time, but not as early as the period that interested her.

Did Holt know about this attic? Perhaps not, since he'd never lived in this house. Certainly, knowing her interests, he would have mentioned it.

At the top of the staircase, Caitlin paused and took a breath while she surveyed the open attic space that had been to the side and behind her as she mounted the stairs. Cobwebs draped from rafters to exposed lightbulbs across the ceiling, dangling down to the attic's contents. Caitlin shuddered. She hated spiders.

Well, there was no way to avoid them other than going back downstairs for a broom. She moved into the space, gaze drawn by a grouping of furniture once covered with sheets and now half exposed as old fabric rotted and split apart. She ducked under a low-hanging cobweb but managed to catch some of it in her hair. "Shite!" she cried, batting at it and shuddering. At least she didn't see any creepie-crawlies...yet.

Straightening, she fingered the fabric. Linen, yellowed by time. She flipped up a corner to expose a sideboard and coughed as dust filled the air. She turned away and breathed through the fabric of her sleeve until the dust settled. Next time, she'd bring a broom and a dust mask with her. But while she was here...she turned back to the sideboard and studied it.

Older than the showpieces downstairs, not as finely crafted. The finish had darkened almost to black. The linen might have blocked some of the dust, but not all of it. She ran her finger across the top and left a revealing streak of woodgrain.

Next, she tugged at a drawer. It slid open with a squeal of protest, then got stuck halfway. She couldn't see anything inside it and made a mental note to add a torch— a flashlight on this side of the Atlantic— to the list of things to carry up the stairs next time. Another drawer wouldn't budge, but one below it slid open smoothly. As near as she could see, it too was empty, but she hesitated to put her hand in and feel for contents. Something might have taken up residence in there. Instead, she pushed it closed and lifted more of the linen out of the way, revealing a side table tucked between the sideboard and a headboard.

They all looked to be of an age, darkened by time, of simple lines and graceless construction. Crouching down, she tugged the small table out into the light. Square, with four square legs and one drawer, there was nothing fancy about it. It might have been used as a place to put a water pitcher or washbowl in someone's chamber or stood beside a chair. During a later time, it would have boasted inlaid wood, cabriole legs, or a center column with three curved feet, an ogee edge on the top surface and a metal or glass drawer pull. Not this poor wee thing. This was much rougher stuff, this wee table. Possibly older than the showpieces downstairs…or just cheaper.

Caitlin left it and pulled the linen away from the piece behind the headboard. Another cabinet, taller than the sideboard she uncovered first, but still rough, with several columns of small drawers. Serviceable, not decorative. Something from servants' quarters, she mused. Or used in a kitchen or apothecary? Interesting for its history, but she doubted it would prove to be very valuable. Still, in this light, it was hard to tell. She turned to head back to the stairs, still thinking she'd come back up later, with her list of items and something to add to the illumination, and walked right into a dangling cobweb.

Shrieking and batting at the gossamer threads like a madwoman, she backed away, knowing if she darted toward the stairs, she might run into another and find one inhabited.

At first, she thought she heard her heart pounding in fear, then realized she was hearing footsteps pounding the floor below her and up the stairs, while she fought to clear the mess from her face.

"Caitlin, what the hell?"

"Help!"

For a change, Holt's laugh didn't please her. And it certainly didn't help the situation. She stopped thrashing long enough to glare at him out of the one eye she'd managed to uncover. "Are you going to help me or not? There might be spiders!"

Holt moved toward her, his grin widening the closer he got. At the moment, she couldn't enjoy it.

"Nope, no spiders."

"Nay?" Caitlin's hands fell to her sides, and her shoulders dropped, then she went back to trying to clear away the mess. "How…?"

"According to some of the paperwork I've been reading, an exterminator sprayed up here last month," Holt told her while he helped pull sticky strands from her face and hair. "These cobwebs are probably as old as the Jacobite stuff you're interested in, though how he avoided them is a mystery."

Caitlin sighed in relief that she wasn't going to die by spider bite. Or was she? "Maybe the exterminator didn't do what the paperwork claimed." Only then did she become aware of how good Holt's hands felt brushing her skin, his fingers plucking at her hair, her cheek, her throat. Her pulse ratcheted up again.

"Here, let me get that," Holt said, grasping her hand and moving it out of the way so he could remove a long strand of a spider's web lying across her nose and down her cheek. "How did you manage to walk into a web?"

Caitlin forced herself to focus on what Holt said, not what he was doing. "I was thinking about what I needed to bring up here and not paying attention." Heat climbed her throat again. He must think her daft. She gestured upward. "A broom moved to the top of my list."

"No doubt." He tugged at her hair, then nodded. "There. I think that's most of it. The rest will wash out."

Caitlin shuddered.

"So, you're not fond of spiders?"

She planted her fists on her hips. "If you laugh again, I'll bloody well shove you into one of these and see how you like it."

Holt held up both hands, palms out. "Truce." He glanced around. "Now, tell me what you found up here." His lips quirked at one corner. "Other than cobwebs, that is."

Caitlin muttered a Gaelic curse under her breath, then gestured toward the furniture grouping. "Nothing much—yet. I need a good torch…flashlight…and some lamps, among other things, to be able to see much of these. Hence my list."

"Of course."

"Where have you been today? And how was your trip to the city?"

"Out and about. I'll tell you later." Holt took her hand and tugged her toward the stairs. "Let's gather what you need and leave it at the bottom of the stairs. I'll help you carry it up after dinner. To make up for laughing at your predicament."

"If that's an apology, I accept it."

"Good enough."

~

Holt stared at himself in the bathroom mirror, where he'd gone to clean up before dinner after helping Caitlin gather what she thought she needed. He almost didn't recognize the man he saw there. Where were the grim expression, the tight shoulders, the down-turned mouth? He didn't understand what was happening to him. In the space of a few days, his whole world seemed brighter. He realized that while he enjoyed simple meals, simple tasks, and verbal sparring with Caitlin Paterson, he'd forgotten all about his company's problems, the aggravation of taking Helen to court, and his antipathy toward the estate.

Caitlin challenged him. Entertained him. Attracted him. Influenced him to the point of seeking out his past and enjoying time with some old friends, even though he'd sworn to get here, focus on selling this place, and get out as fast as he could. He glanced around the bathroom and out the open door into the bedroom. Somehow, none of that seemed as urgent as it once had.

Rescuing Caitlin from imagined spiders was the most

fun he'd had since the wave dunked her and he'd rescued her from the ocean. Peeling sticky webs and brushing dust from her hair had given him the excuse to touch her face, her throat— caresses that seemed somehow more intimate than carrying her cradled against his chest or tending to a cut on her foot. He swallowed, imaging putting his hands on her lush body anywhere she'd allow— teasing her just to hear her laugh. He wanted to know everything about her. He suddenly realized he didn't want to lose her to Scotland or for her to be far, far away from where he lived and worked.

This was bad.

He'd just won the case against Helen. She'd had no case, but she hadn't accepted her lawyer's advice. So she'd been forced to listen to his lawyer and witnesses refute every claim she made and confirm Holt's. Once it was over, his lawyer advised him he had grounds to sue her for libel, slander, and a whole host of workplace violations, but Holt didn't have the heart to drag her through any more mud than she'd already splashed on herself. He understood she'd moved to Texas somewhere. He hoped she'd learned her lesson.

He'd learned one, too. Don't go socially anywhere near a female in a professional relationship. Of course, Caitlin wasn't his employee. He was her client. That gave him some latitude to chip away at his reserve— and hers— to get her interested in him as a person, which seemed to be happening. With Mrs. Smith going out of her way to make dinners and lunches and breakfasts as homey as possible, going so far as to share meals with them in the kitchen rather than consigning them to the small dining room, this was far from a standard workplace environment.

Still, he'd better take a step back, enjoy the time they had together, but not expect more from Caitlin, no matter how much he wanted it.

He wondered how long his resolve would last.

CHAPTER 7

Thanks to a business call that kept Holt occupied after dinner, Caitlin didn't get back up to the attic until the next morning. Farrell preceded her, wielding a broom like a sorcerer's wand, wiping away the cobwebs that had terrorized her yesterday. Finally, when the only remnants left were high in the eaves out of reach, Caitlin thanked him, and he headed back down the stairs, carefully avoiding the heavy-duty extension cord Holt had dragged up earlier.

Holt came up then and plugged in the lamps he had brought up while Caitlin finished her breakfast, spread them out in a rough circle as far as their cords would reach and stood back, waiting for her assessment.

"Perfect," Caitlin told him. "That gives me a bright area to work within."

"What else do you need?"

Hands on hips, Caitlin surveyed the space. While what she'd seen the day before didn't look terribly promising, she knew better than to make assumptions. Some of the most attractive pieces were the least valuable and vice versa. Everything came down to provenance, history, even sentimental value. Until she'd carefully examined everything up here, she'd reserve judgment.

Much less scary now that light reached all the way to its walls, the attic took on more manageable dimensions, and the light revealed pieces she'd missed. She took a step toward a tallboy secretary, then stopped when she spotted a low, dark shape. "Look! There's a trunk. Help me move that over here first." With an evil grin, she added, "In my experience, ye never ken what treasures a trunk might hold."

Holt didn't comment until they stood over it. Then he ran a finger across the top, leaving a streak in the dust coating it. "If it held treasure, someone would have emptied it by now."

Age had darkened the center metal lock plate to the point Caitlin couldn't be sure if it was originally brass or steel or something else. The painted wooden sides lacked carry straps, so she braced her hands on either side and tried lifting. The trunk didn't budge. "It looks like a late 19th-century travel trunk— the kind people used for long trips on trains or ships, but I'll know more when we open it. It's heavy, so there's something in it. Will any of the lights reach over here so we don't have to move it?"

Instead of trying to lift it, Holt gave it a shove. It budged, but only a little. "I guess we'll have to. It appears to be full of rocks."

"Or gold?"

"Or lead," he replied then moved as many lights as he could to create a half-circle of illumination around the front of the chest.

While he did that, Caitlin flicked on the torch and moved the beam over the entire front surface. Careful of the things stacked around the chest, she picked her way to the other side and examined the back as well. The hinges appeared to be in good shape, and she didn't see any obvious damage.

"That'll have to do," Holt finally said. "Let's open it."

"Not so fast." She moved back to the front, knelt by Holt and shone the torchlight on the lock plate. "We don't have a key. I don't suppose you're any good at picking locks."

"Not one of my many talents, sorry. As old as this looks, we could probably break into it pretty easily."

Caitlin shook her head. "Nay. We don't know how old this is. The trunk might have value of its own, more if it's intact." She sat back on her heels. "Before you got here from California, I found a ring of keys in your great-aunt's chamber. Perhaps one of those..."

Holt stood. "Where?"

"In her dresser, bottom drawer, back right corner, I believe." She'd looked at and into so many pieces of furniture since she'd arrived, she hoped she remembered the right drawer and wasn't sending Holt on a fruitless search.

While he was gone, she took pictures of the trunk and the surfaces of a few other pieces the light reached, and then she moved further into the recesses of the attic. A wrought-iron headboard leaned against one wall, the tops of its curved posts visible above a stack of pasteboard boxes. A good home for insects, Caitlin thought, like the spiders responsible for those ghastly cobwebs. But perhaps they contained old dishes or something else of value. A set of metal shelves held bits and bobs—broken crockery, lamp parts, even a few bolts of fabric she recognized as having been used for the draperies downstairs.

"Ordered too much, did ye?" she muttered as she swept the light over the next shelf.

A small wooden box caught her eye. For jewels? Or fishing lures. One never kenned until one opened it. She reached for it but heard the stairs groaning under Holt's heavy tread as keys clinked in time with each step. So she returned to the trunk, their primary focus at the moment.

"Found them," Holt announced as he crested the stairs. He held the keyring aloft and shook it, making the keys rattle together.

Caitlin took the ring from him and flipped keys aside as she studied each one. "Four of these look like modern house keys, but one of the smaller ones might be what we need." She knelt and gently inserted one after the other, some fitting better than others, but none releasing the lock. "Damn." Caitlin sank back on her heels and thought. "I haven't found any other key rings in the pieces I've cataloged, but there might be more kept where other keys are used, like in the kitchen."

"Why would anyone keep the key to something like this in the kitchen?"

Caitlin shrugged. "They wouldn't, not usually. If the

keys were for something special, they'd hide them, or at least put them out of sight, as your great-aunt did."

"Let me try them." Holt held out his hand, palm up. "Maybe the lock needs more encouragement."

Caitlin handed over the keys and scooted out of the way. "Try not to break it, please."

Holt fitted the first key and attempted to turn it in both directions, to no avail. He inserted it upside down and repeated the procedure, then moved on to the next key and the next. Finally, something clicked and the key turned. Holt caught the hinged lock plate as it fell open, then turned to Caitlin with a grin. "We're in."

Caitlin took a moment to appreciate Holt's enjoyment of his success. He'd opened up to her so much in the last few days, she hoped his change of heart would continue. Then she nodded and flipped open one catch as Holt opened the other. She grasped the lid's corners and paused again. What were they about to find?

"Well?" Holt gestured for her to open it.

"Just taking a second to appreciate the moment," she scolded. "Whatever is in here could change your life."

"Or be a box of rocks," Holt replied and gestured *up*.

Nodding, Caitlin lifted the lid, the hinges creaking as it moved.

"Needs a bit of WD-40," Holt remarked.

Caitlin didn't bother to answer. She was entranced by what the chest revealed. Stacks of stereographic prints, and wrapped in muslin that she carefully unfolded, the stereoscope used to view them.

"Old postcards?" Holt asked, derision in his tone.

"Ye have never seen these? Or their like before?"

He shook his head. "What are they?"

She examined the viewer before lifting it to show Holt. It appeared to be in perfect condition. "This is called a stereoscope. Put any of these stereograph cards in here," she said, pointing to the slot they fit into, "look through the eyepiece, and the two images become one 3-D view."

"No kidding." He reached into the trunk for a card.

Caitlin slapped his hand away. "Don't! Don't touch them. No' yet. I dinna ken what condition they're in. The paper might fall to bits." She held up a hand as he looked ready to object. "Just wait."

She set the stereoscope back on its bed of muslin, then dug her cotton gloves out of her back pocket and donned them. The corner of the top stereograph felt solid and didn't stick to the one below it when she shifted it. She slid her hand under and picked it up, then moved it into the nearby lamp's light. It showed a street scene, carriages and horses, mostly, with a few men in garb from another century.

Confident now that the card wouldn't fall apart, she placed it into the stereoscope and looked through the viewfinder. Protected from dust by its wrapping and the trunk, the lenses were clear.

Smiling, she passed it to Holt. "Take a look."

∼

Holt had never seen a contraption like this one, but he had to hand it to its creators. It did just what Caitlin described. The card with two images became one with depth and detail. He studied the carts and the clothes the men wore, trying to place the image in time. "How old is it?"

"I'll have to examine it, and the pictures stored with it, but I'd guess it's Victorian or Edwardian. Nineteenth century to early twentieth to you Yanks. The viewer was invented in the early nineteenth century."

"I wonder how long it's been sitting in this attic," Holt remarked, handing the viewer back to her.

Caitlin replaced the card in the stack and tucked the cloth wrapping around the viewer. "No telling. But these pictures might tell us more about your family's background, or at least about what interested your ancestors."

If they weren't worth much, Holt wasn't sure he cared. "So, not rocks," he prompted.

"Nay. But perhaps something quite valuable, I think, at least to the right collector."

Good. Someone might buy the lot. "Or a museum?"

"Doubtful. These were quite common until the mid-twentieth century when they couldn't compete with modern photography or later, entertainment such as television. Their value will be in the uniqueness of the images, I'd say."

Holt surprised himself by spending the rest of the morning, once Caitlin forced him to don a pair of cotton gloves, going through stacks of stereographs, helping her photograph and sort them. He'd found a small rectangular table at the other end of the attic and moved it into the circle of lights, giving her an adequate, she said, workspace. Her detailed notes impressed him, both with the seriousness with which she approached the investigation, and her apparent competence. Any lingering uncertainty about why the estate's executor had hired her vanished over the course of the morning.

Eventually, a loud growl from the region of his stomach reminded him they'd been at this for hours, so Holt called a halt. "Let's get some lunch. You need a break."

"Speak for yourself." Caitlin's stomach chose that moment to answer the growl his had made. She blushed and quirked an eyebrow, then set aside her notebook and the stereograph she'd been studying, stretched her arms over her head, and stood, looking anywhere but at him. "Yeah, okay. You're right. I guess I am hungry."

The color flooding her cheeks captured Holt's attention. Did she blush like that all over? Pink. No, dusky rose, at least in this light. She'd blushed redder at lunch, but that might have been the malt vinegar she used on her fish and the difference in lighting. He tore his gaze away and gestured toward the stairs. "After you."

Over lunch, Caitlin filled him in on the history of the stereograph, convincing him that in and of itself, it was nothing unusual.

"But I hope to find some interesting and unique images, or images of clear historical value, among the stereographs. I've already found a few possibilities, but going through that trunk is going to take time."

"What can I do to help?"

"I found some old tools and broken bits on a set of metal shelves on the opposite side of the attic. Maybe you could take a look at those and see if there's anything interesting. Tools are not my area of expertise."

Holt couldn't resist the chance to pounce. Payback for all the times she'd lectured him about this house. "Because I'm a guy, you think I'm a tool expert, is that it?" She seemed to enjoy the challenges of her profession. She wouldn't be able to resist if he challenged her in other ways.

Caitlin paused with her sandwich halfway from her plate to her mouth. "I never said—"

"No, you assumed. Don't they call that gender bias now?" He was tempted to grin, to soften the implied criticism, but he wanted to get a rise out of her. She was too professional, too set on doing her job. He wanted her to have the same sense of enjoyment he'd felt yesterday reconnecting with old friends, then rescuing her from spider webs. Enjoyment she seemed to have, and he lacked, their first few days here. Funny how their moods had reversed. A little teasing seemed in order.

Grimly, Caitlin set down her sandwich and met his gaze. "I am one of the foremost experts on late medieval to Jacobean furnishings. That doesn't make me an expert on everything likely to be found in a dusty, cobwebby old attic on the other side of the Atlantic. Since you asked what you could do to help, I'd have asked you to take a look at those shelves, whether you were male or female or from another planet."

Her voice had increased in volume as she spoke, but then she pulled her napkin from her lap and tossed it on the table, muttering something under her breath that sounded like *Does he think me head zips up in the back?* That couldn't be right. But she did look furious. No, insulted. Holt decided a tactical retreat was in order. "Okay, okay. I was kidding." He held up both hands, palms out. "I'm not questioning your competence. I was making a joke. A poor one. Not funny. I get it. Finish your lunch. Please." Getting a rise out of her was one thing. Pissing her off to the point that she stormed out again, or worse, decided she'd had enough of him and quit, was just damn stupid.

To his great relief, Caitlin replaced her napkin across her lap and picked up her sandwich, though her eyes still sparked when she glanced his way. What he needed was a change of subject. Like now. While she was chewing.

"So, the people in those images, do you think they're related? To me?"

Caitlin shrugged and swallowed. "Maybe. I dinna ken how we'd ever prove it, though, unless someone wrote names and dates on the backs of some of the card framing the pictures. Like as not they'd no' write directly opposite the image for fear of ink bleeding through."

Holt had noticed that the more emotional Caitlin got, the thicker her Scottish brogue became. She was still angry. He wasn't out of the hole he'd dug for himself yet.

"We haven't looked at all of them," Caitlin continued, frowning, "but I noticed a lot of single people. Or one adult with only one or two children. Not many couples, none of the big families that would have been more common during that time. I do wonder why that is."

A frisson of awareness ran along Holt's spine, tightening his muscles and making him draw his brows together. He dropped his gaze to the table, unable to look at Caitlin while uneasiness chilled his blood. In the novelty of his experiences since he'd arrived here— and his growing attraction to the woman sitting across from him— he'd nearly forgotten about this aspect of his family history. Could they have been looking at proof of the family curse all morning? Proof he had failed to notice? As much as he wanted to laugh it off, his mother had sworn the curse was real. The only way to be sure was to find some names or find another way to identify some of the people in those stereographs.

"Holt?"

Caitlin's voice jerked him back to the real world, and he looked up. "I don't know. Or maybe I do."

"What do you mean?"

He crossed his arms. "My mother used to insist the family was cursed."

"You're joking again, and again, not funny." Caitlin regarded him under lowered brows.

"No, I'm not." He heaved a sigh, resolved to give her the whole crazy story. "She swore that earlier generations of the family had only one or two children and that no heir found a love that lasted their lifetime. In every generation, the heir or their spouse left. Or died. Or somehow disappeared, never to be heard from again. None grew old together."

"Did your great-aunt have children?"

"No, none. My grandfather, her younger brother, was her heir. Had he outlived her, all this would have been his, then my mother's, then wound up as mine." Which might also explain his great-aunt's bequest, to repair the line of succession. "But he didn't outlive her. Unfortunately, since she named me heir, there must not have been any other family on her husband's side to inherit, or to carry the curse, so my grandfather's line acquired it. My mother's parents died. She was left alone…with me, an only child."

Caitlin leaned back and regarded him, disbelief plain in her furrowed brow. "And your father disappeared…"

"Exactly. Before my mother told him about me. Before she even knew about me. She told me once my father was dead, too."

"I'm so sorry. What happened to your grandmother? Did she leave your grandfather?"

"In a way. She died long before him, after giving birth to my mother."

"*Ach*, Holt. What a sad tale."

"If you believe in the curse, it could explain a lot. And if it's true, any woman foolish enough to marry me will die after giving me an heir, or divorce me, or disappear into the Bermuda Triangle." She needed to know that. It should send her running back to Scotland all the faster. He wanted to laugh it off, but those pictures… He fought a shudder. "Those sad faces, adults' and children's, have begun to haunt me. Ghosts of Christmases past, I suppose."

Caitlin reached over and grasped his hand. "Ye canna

think that way. It may just be an old tale. Like fairies and ghosts and goblins."

Then she paused, and Holt swore the color fled her face for just a moment, then came back even stronger, painting her neck and cheeks in that lovely dusky rose. "What's wrong?"

"Would ye believe me if I told ye I have seen a ghost? Many times? We have them in Scotland, aye." She smiled wistfully at that, then became serious again. "And curses, too, or so the grannies say."

Holt pressed his lips together. "No, I wouldn't believe you— or I don't want to. I'm sure of that."

Caitlin squeezed his hand, then removed hers and crossed her arms, frowning at her empty plate. "Well, if we're going to get to the bottom of this, we'll no' do it sitting at table. Are ye done?"

With his food, yes. With her touch and the heat that simple connection created, no. But the same unwelcome thought coiled in his belly like a snake, fangs dripping poison. He couldn't get involved with her. If the curse was real, she could die.

~

Hours later, Caitlin stood, stretched her arms above her head, and then rubbed her eyes. With Holt's help, she'd emptied the chest of its hoard of images and examined them, one by one. Holt had given up about halfway through, convinced there were no answers to be found, and tired of wasting his time when he had real work to do.

Stung, she knew her frustration could not match his— he had a greater reason for it— but she had been sure they would find something in the hundreds of stereographs his great-aunt, or someone before her, had saved. As much as she loved solving a mystery— which she did with every piece of furniture she appraised— this one worried her, if only because Holt, despite his denials, seemed to take the idea of a curse seriously. Well, she hoped some answers would turn up soon.

In the meantime, she needed to get out of this dark attic and take a walk. She checked the time on her phone. Another half hour until sunset. A short walk then, and a chance to give her eyes something distant to focus on. She turned off the desk and other lights and made her way down the stairs to her room to grab a coat, hat, and gloves, then went outside.

Her first breath of cold air nearly sent her back indoors, but the lowering sun had painted the broken clouds to the west in shades of gold and crimson, pink and purple, that lit the remains of earlier snows in watercolor streaks. She stepped off the porch onto the circular drive, her gaze on the sky.

"Where are you going?"

The sound of Holt's voice made her whip around. She'd been so focused on the sunset, she hadn't heard the door open and close. "Having a walk," she replied, more breathless than she expected, surely from the cold and not from Holt's sudden arrival. "And a chance to rest my eyes."

He was pulling on a jacket as he approached her. A knitted scarf hung loosely around his neck. He tucked the scarf inside the jacket as he buttoned it.

She was happy to rest her eyes on him.

"Want some company?"

"Sure." She realized she was staring and turned back to the west. "Look at that sky!"

Holt came up beside her, and out of the corner of her eye, she saw him nod.

"Sunsets like that are rare in winter. Let's enjoy it while we walk." He took her hand and led her toward the setting sun, old snow and frozen grass crunching under their boots. They crossed the lawn for a better view as the sun sank between some trees. Caitlin felt her muscles loosening as she moved, welcomed relief from the tension caused by hours of sitting and concentrating.

"Still didn't find anything?"

She knew her answer would disappoint him. "Nay. Lots of interesting images, but no names or dates penciled on the back."

"Interesting? How?"

"How much do ye ken about the Victorian era?"

Holt stared at the sky, then took a breath. "I've got nothing."

"Well, Queen Victoria loved spending time in Scotland. She's the reason the royal family has the Balmoral estate in Scotland today. Her husband, Prince Albert, bought it for her, a private sale, so rather than belonging to the Crown, it belongs to the family. Anyway, all things tartan became popular during her reign. Many of the images in those stereographs toward the bottom of the trunk are of men in plaid clothing, even in kilts. I'd wager they're not Scots, but it's possible."

"What time period are you talking about?"

"Nineteenth century. Her reign lasted 60 years, until 1901. Those images may indicate the age of many of those stereographs."

"I don't see how that helps us."

"I'm not certain it does." She sighed and forced her focus back to the sunset, now dimming, colors fading into the gloaming. "I wish I had answers for you."

Holt shrugged. "Finding that trunk was a fluke. I don't think it had been touched in decades, maybe not since the beginning of the last century. There's no reason it would provide answers to anything."

As the sky darkened, fairy lights popped on in the white-painted gazebo set in the middle of the side lawn.

"How lovely," Caitlin exclaimed. "Let's go over there."

Holt frowned, then gestured for her to lead the way. The untrodden snow was deeper on this side of the house, up to Caitlin's ankles. She walked carefully, on the lookout for icy patches that might have formed as the day's melting refroze. Holt lagged a step behind her, ready, she suspected, to catch her if she slipped. But she reached the gazebo without incident and mounted the two steps to the interior. Inside, the fairy lights cast a warm glow that bled onto the surrounding snow. A row of benches circled the outside edge, and the roof rose to a pointed peak. Carved columns and fancy gingerbread, all painted white, supported the roof and provided a sense of cozy enclosure.

Holt crossed to the side that the roof had protected from the last snowfall. "The bench is dry over here if you want to sit down."

Caitlin joined him. "This is such a magical spot on a lovely estate. You're lucky to have inherited it."

"Appearances can be deceiving," Holt replied, his expression grim as he looked around. "My mother loved this spot. She told me after she got pregnant with me and her aunt kicked her out, she thought she'd never be able to set foot here again."

"I'm sorry she was treated so unfairly." Caitlin couldn't imagine treating someone that way.

"There's more. When I was very young, Mother drove me past here, pointing out where she'd come from and that we were not welcome. I'd always thought the house was haunted…but not this…" He indicated the gazebo. "It was pretty, and she loved it. I begged her to sneak over here when we knew my great-aunt was out of town, so I could find out. I thought it would be a grand adventure. Mother finally brought me when I was about nine."

"That was kind of ye to give her a reason to return."

He shook his head. "You know what they say about good intentions. It was a sunny summer day with a cooling breeze off the water, puffy clouds scudding across the sky, and every plant on the estate in full flower."

"Magical."

"Then, the wicked witch showed up."

"*Ach*, nay." Suddenly, the twinkly lights held no warmth.

"Returned early from wherever she'd ridden her broom," Holt continued. "Mother heard her voice and tried to hustle us away before her aunt found out we were there, but she spotted us."

He took a breath as if gathering strength to keep the story going. Caitlin was tempted to stop him, but she suspected this was a tale he'd carried within himself for years. Curiosity got the best of her, and she stayed silent, waiting for him to add the rest of what he needed to say.

"The scene that followed cemented my…distaste…for that woman and this place." Holt paused and looked around, his gaze tracking to the peak of the roof. "I'll never forget my mother's tears when her aunt appeared. She reinforced my childish notion that only evil spirits could make someone treat my mother so badly."

He needed a minute. She could see it in the sudden glint in his eyes, as if looking up would stop any tears that threatened. She'd been right that this was something he'd never shared, never exposed to the light of day, and to do it here, in the place where it happened, had to be excruciating. Brave. Perhaps even heartrending. The Holt she'd first met would never have exposed such vulnerability. She felt honored that he shared this much with her. "Why did your mother make you aware of her background? Had you asked?"

"Probably." Holt leaned forward and rested his elbows on his knees, his gaze on his feet. "I was a precocious child. My intellect and curiosity constantly got me in trouble. That day, it backfired big time." Then he straightened. "The way my great-aunt reacted to our presence, I'm surprised she didn't have this structure burned down."

Caitlin stood. "I'm so sorry. We should go. I never should have insisted we come out here."

Holt grasped her gloved hand, making her wish she could feel the warmth of his skin. "You had no way of knowing about my past. Sit down and enjoy the present," he said, tugging. "It all happened a long time ago."

Caitlin sat. It was that or be pulled off her feet onto his lap. "But it still hurts. I hear it in your voice." And she regretted being the reason for it.

"I'm a big boy now. I can handle it." But his gaze was still turned inward.

Caitlin pulled her hand free and stood. "Ye shouldn't have to." When he didn't budge, she added, "Besides, I'm getting cold. Let's go in."

Holt leaned against the column at his back, then blew out a breath, met her gaze, and stood. "You're right, the wind is picking up. Let's go in."

Caitlin headed for the mansion. The warm yellow light spilling from its windows beckoned her. But she now had a better idea why Holt saw this place very differently than she did. Appearances *could* be deceiving.

CHAPTER 8

Holt couldn't believe he'd shared that story. It had to be the place, if not the time or season, and the woman beside him. Caitlin's sympathy and understanding had loosened the knots holding back his memories— his feelings— and they'd spilled out. He regretted spoiling her enjoyment of the gazebo, but perhaps it was just as well. Maybe now she'd stop trying to convince him of the appeal the estate. He didn't understand why she seemed so determined that he keep it. Live in it, for God's sake, as if he'd ever do that. Staying here for a few weeks was bad enough, though his temporary residence kept him out of county court. Still, he couldn't wait to get back to California. The only downside to that plan walked quietly at his side.

He helped her up the stairs onto the front portico then held the front door open. Her scent teased him, wafting past him on the warm air spilling out of the house and stirring his blood. She touched his glove as she brushed by, and he remembered that all too soon, like her brief touch, she'd be gone. She was here to do a job, he told himself as he helped her remove her coat, then stripped out of his. Farrell appeared in time to take charge of them, along with their hats, gloves, and scarves. He announced that hot cocoa awaited their pleasure in the kitchen. Holt followed Caitlin down the richly paneled hallway where the scent of chocolate and something else grew stronger with each step. He reminded himself as he went that the estate was a job site, nothing more, its contents merely items to be assessed, cataloged, and disposed of. As soon as she finished, and as soon as he dealt with the lawyers, the county tax office, and a wealth of other details, he'd sell the place and never set foot in it again.

Then she would go back to Scotland, and he'd likely never see her again, despite his teasing threat to show up at her door. He'd had this thought before. The kick to his gut got stronger each time. He wanted to grab her shoulders and stop her, lean down and whisper in her ear that he didn't want to lose her, but he didn't know what to do about it. Then turn her to face him and kiss her. He didn't. Nor could he say anything like that. Neither of them were ready to deal with what it might mean, or how it would change the fragile friendship they now shared, and that surprised the hell out of him. The friendship that Caitlin had coaxed him into, truth be told, by doing her best to help him. And by just being herself. He never thought such a thing would be possible ever again. Did he really want to risk losing it? Losing her even before their lives forced them apart? He knew the answer, even if he didn't want to admit it to himself— or to her.

Holt squinted as they entered the brightly lit kitchen.

Caitlin took a deep breath and sighed. "Ah, chocolate," she said with a smile for Mrs. Smith. "Ye're an angel to think of this," she added as Mrs. Smith handed her a steaming mug.

"I saw the two of you outside at sunset and knew you'd be chilled by the time you came back in."

"You were right," Holt assured her as he took charge of his own steaming mug, then took a cautious sip. Hot, creamy, almost smoky, the cocoa satisfied a need for comfort he hadn't known he could feel so deeply. Today was a day for revelations, he mused, and most of them hurt. But not all.

"This is amazing," Caitlin exclaimed after a few sips. "You must tell me your secret. What's in it?"

Mrs. Smith waved a hand. "It's my special recipe I only make during the holidays. I use Mexican chocolate, which has cinnamon and a touch of cayenne to warm it."

Of course, Holt thought. "I've had something like this in California. I should have recognized it…"

"I want the recipe," Caitlin interrupted with enthusiasm. "I've never tasted the like. I'm sure my friends at home would adore this."

Mrs. Smith beamed. "I'll write it out for you and make sure we have a good supply of the chocolate to send home with you."

Holt's gut clenched at Mrs. Smith's innocent offer, an

echo of his recent thoughts that made Caitlin's departure seem that much more imminent and inevitable.

"Would you care for more?"

With a smile, Caitlin held out her mug. "Aye, of course!"

Mrs. Smith ladled out more fragrant chocolate and topped off Caitlin's mug, then Holt's. "Have a seat at the kitchen table. I've been cooking all day, so this is the warmest room in the house. I'll just leave you to it and come back later to clean up and get dinner on the table."

"Thank you," Holt replied and waited until she left the room. He took a seat next to Caitlin and thawed his hands around his mug.

"This warms me all the way through," Caitlin told him. "It's going to be very popular back home."

"A worthwhile souvenir of your trip," he quipped but left unspoken his sudden recognition of how unhappy the idea of her leaving made him, or the other, more pleasurable ways he'd like to warm her in the meantime.

"Mrs. Smith and Farrell are treasures," she said. "I'm going to miss them."

He pictured her sitting with friends in front of a peat fire, sipping Mrs. Smith's chocolate and realized if that actually happened, if he weren't there, too, he'd never be able to drink spiced chocolate again without missing her. With every sip, her cheeks pinked, and her eyes closed in obvious bliss. How he'd enjoy being the one to put that expression on her face, to watch a flush of color rise from her chest to her eyes. Damn it, he had to stop thinking this way. But her sweater hugged enticing curves, and her hair fell across her forehead, making him long to brush it back, then run his fingers down the graceful length of her throat while he kissed her.

They sipped in silence for a few minutes, then Caitlin set her mug aside and frowned. "I'm really sorry, about… before. I can't imagine how awful it must have been for you and your mother to be chased away from here. No room at the inn…." She trailed off with a frown, then shrugged and continued, "Even though it was summer and not Yuletide."

Holt struggled for words. He'd been too young to go to his mother's defense, but old enough to understand most of the invectives her aunt hurled at her. To see the anger and hurt and shame in her eyes as she tried to shield him from the scene.

"I have never forgotten my mother insisting I was not a mistake. At the time, I didn't know what she meant, not really. Certainly my mother never treated me in any way that suggested she didn't want me. Though her life would have been much simpler, much better, and perhaps much longer without me."

"Holt! Nay."

"I don't know for certain, but I expect my great-aunt forbade my mother from seeing my father. He wasn't from a good— in her estimation— family. Wrong social strata altogether."

"How awful for her. And then to find out she was pregnant…"

"Years later, long after we were chased away from here, Mother told me her aunt kicked her out as soon as she started showing."

"I see why you never wanted to come back here."

"And why I'm eager to get rid of this place. Family curse aside, for my mother and me it was and is full of unhappy memories." So why did the gazebo now appear in his thoughts with Caitlin glowing in the fairly lights rather than the painful daytime image of his great-aunt snarling threats at his mother?

Caitlin drummed her fingers on the tabletop, a nervous gesture he'd never seen her indulge in before. Holt wanted to reach over and take her hand, to soothe away her disquiet. But touching her would do nothing to soothe him. So he stayed still and let her think.

"I want to pull the drawers out of that apothecary cabinet," she finally said, a change of topic so abrupt, he didn't understand her for a moment.

"Apothecary cabinet?"

"That's what I'm calling it. The one with rows and rows of small, square drawers. Tomorrow morning, let's drag it into the circle of light and see what there is to see."

"Why that piece?"

"I could say because it's the next nearest and we don't have to move anything else out of the way to get to it, but I have this feeling…"

"Feeling?"

"We Scots women put a lot of stock in our feelings." She straightened and grinned. "We come from a long line of seers, Druids, that sort of thing."

Holt laughed, and Caitlin quickly joined in. She'd been teasing. Well, she'd succeeded in lightening the mood, if that had been her intention in changing the subject from his painful past. He was glad she cared enough to try.

"Then we'll do as you say," Holt promised, wondering if, behind her teasing, there was a bit of truth. The glint in her eyes said yes.

~

The next morning, Caitlin grabbed a small notepad and black marker pen before she went upstairs. Careful to avoid the heavy-duty extension cord running up the stairs, she made the climb to the attic. Holt was already there and had wrestled the apothecary cabinet into the open space closest to where it had been and arranged their lights around it.

Her granny might have had a good Gaelic word for the feeling that filled Caitlin when Holt talked about his family. All Caitlin knew was that Holt's story felt like a portent. For him, and perhaps, given the ice that had skittered down her spine, for her, too. She knew her decision to tackle the apothecary cabinet had thrown Holt, but though she wasn't sure why it had seemed so important, in that moment, she had acquired a quest. Even though he'd once told her he didn't want her meddling in his personal life, they were well beyond that now. She needed to discover what she could about Holt's family, the curse he'd mentioned and tried to scoff at, and his missing father. She'd told Holt the truth. She had a feeling about the apothecary cabinet. *A Scottish feeling*. She wouldn't wait any longer to examine it.

"Good morning," she greeted him, glad to see him taking an active interest in the attic's contents. She waved a hand at the cabinet and lights around it. "You were up early."

"I had to be to get here before you. Eager to reveal its secrets?" He hooked a thumb toward the chest.

After setting her burdens down on a nearby tabletop, Caitlin quirked an eyebrow. "Apparently, I'm not the only one. Did you move that by yourself?"

"I could say yes, but I'd be lying. I didn't want to risk damaging it, so I recruited Farrell's help." Holt shrugged. "You did say you had a feeling about this piece."

"I did. I still do. Thank you for being careful with it. But you'll have to be patient a few minutes longer." She bent over the table and tore off single sheets from her notepad, then numbered each one until she had enough for each drawer. "That cabinet is so old, the drawers may fit only in their current slot, so I want to make sure each goes back where it belongs."

"Without damaging them," Holt said, clearly understanding her concern.

She opened the top left drawer far enough to slip the number one inside. "Exactly. You can help by putting the numbers in order in the rest of the drawers while I take a look at the back. Don't open them any farther than you need to, to slip the number inside."

"Like you did. But why focus on the back?" Holt took the stack she handed him and turned to the second drawer in the top row. He tugged it gently open and slipped in the number two sheet.

His attention to her concerns impressed her. "I'm going to do this methodically and carefully," Caitlin told him as he closed that drawer, nodded, and reached for the next. "Because of my feeling, ye ken." Satisfied he understood, she grabbed the torch and stepped around the cabinet, moving the light over its sides and back, looking for cracks, gouges, and any other damage. Given its apparent age, it appeared to be in remarkably good shape. A squeak and soft oath alerted her. "Problem?"

Holt was pushing on the rightmost drawer in the row above the base row. "I think I jammed this one. Sorry."

Caitlin joined Holt at the front. "Leave it for now. It's probably warped. Do the last row, and we'll get started."

When Holt finished, Caitlin pulled a few drawers from the top row and set them on the table she'd been using as a workbench. Before she could finish with that row, he asked, "What are you doing? I could have taken them out if I knew that's what you wanted."

She glanced at him, then resumed her task. "I didn't want them out…then. I needed to see how sturdy the outer box was, and to look for problems. Now, I want the drawers out to inspect them, but also to be able to get to the interior." Holt frowned and muttered something about wasted effort that Caitlin chose to ignore. "If you have something else to do, go ahead. I don't need help with the rest of this."

"Okay." He glanced at his watch. "I've got a videoconference with the city in an hour to get ready for." He turned toward the head of the stairs, then turned back. "Call if you need anything."

She didn't bother to look up. "I will."

"Or scream if you see any spiders."

Caitlin planted her hands on her hips and answered his grin with the glare she used on her cousin Ian's adopted twins when they were trying to pull something over on her. "Again, not funny."

With a smirk, he went down the steps.

Caitlin watched him go, enjoying the way his shoulders moved as he descended, and the wave in his hair, picked out by the light coming up the stairs from the room below. His grin, so rarely displayed, had captivated her, but as Holt disappeared from view, she knew she'd better get back to work. By the time he finished his call, he'd want to know what progress she'd made. Sitting up here thinking about his smile, his shoulders, his— nay, she had to stop. Determined, she turned back to the cabinet and put Holt out of her mind. She finished pulling all the drawers, stacking them on the worktable to study later for variations in construction, materials, size, weight, wear, and so forth. But first, she wanted to know what shining her torch into the interior of the cabinet could tell her.

She didn't notice anything unusual in its construction. And fortunately, no critters had taken up residence. She smelled old wood and dust, nothing more. Scents of previously stored herbs or spices had long since faded. Each cubbyhole was large enough for her hand, so starting with the top row, she reached in and felt for loose framing, rotting wood, or insect damage. Often, she would find things that way, things that were not easily seen by the naked eye. She risked splinters, but some discoveries were worth a little discomfort. Still, everything seemed remarkably uniform for hand-made furniture, until she reached the space where the drawer stuck when Holt tried to close it.

She might have missed it, but in withdrawing her hand, she scraped the top of the center cubby and felt rough wood, not the smooth plank she'd expected. Crouching down, she shone the bright torch beam at the top of the cubby. She couldn't quite make out the damage there, but the color of the wood seemed off, and she suspected something kept in this drawer had repeatedly scraped the bottom of the shelf above it.

She reached in and traced the gouges with her fingertips. Not parallel. Some ran perpendicular, some at angles. A thrill ran through her, raising goose flesh as she realized what she might be feeling. Writing! Something had been scratched or carved in what felt like a block set into the wood. But what? And how to see it?

She needed a hand mirror. And she'd seen one, but where? She sat back on her heels and thought for a moment. Aye, the great-aunt's chamber. One graced her dressing table. It might be too big, but if so, perhaps Mrs. Smith would know where to find another.

As she headed for the steps, she told herself it might only be a maker's mark in an unusual location, or something on the board from before the cabinet was made. But it might also be more.

Then she smacked her forehead. *Eedjit!* She didn't need a mirror. She turned back to the cabinet and opened the camera on her phone, checked that the flash was on, then slid it into the cubby, held her breath, and took the picture.

Yes! It was writing, but she didn't have all of it. She

tried again, taking several pictures while sliding the phone all the way in and then inching it out. When she finished, she had a set of photos that she could overlay and stitch together. Once they finished uploading to her laptop, she sat at the table and tried to puzzle out the carvings.

French, not Gaelic, which told her either the piece was brought over from France, or the person doing the carving was educated and upper class, though given the type of cabinet and the rough finish, probably not nobility. Truly an apothecary? Or a clan's healer? The carving would give her a clue. She went to work with her photo editing software, and before long, had a clear image of the entire inlaid carving. Its block of wood wasn't a perfectly mortised fit, which was why the drawer stuck. But perhaps by the time the space had been chiseled out of the upper frame, and the carved block set in, the owner no longer cared, knowing the end was near. The lines defining the block's edges were clearly visible, as were the words that someone felt were important enough to hide within this chest hundreds of years ago.

Though she could puzzle out some of it, she opened a translation program and sat back in shock when she read the result.

Steal this safe from Scottish soil and cursed be your poor generations with love, like mine, lost too soon. 1746

Dear God. Holt's mother was right. The family was cursed, and this cabinet was the reason. Caitlin's heart beat a wild staccato in her chest. It made sense that it belonged to a Jacobite family, a Jacobite healer, since she thought it most likely for a woman to pronounce a curse for a love lost too soon— one who'd been lost at Culloden, perhaps?

The cabinet must have been stolen by an English soldier or noble, sent back to England and from there to America generations later— *poor* generations later. In this context, that had to mean poor of children, of descendants. Of a future, with only enough to carry on the family name and the curse. An heir, few more. And love lost too soon. Holt knew his family's tragic history two or three generations back, but she strongly suspected if she could trace it into the late 1700s, the same pattern would appear. The 19th century Christmas stereographic pictures of one adult with one or two children certainly fit.

There was only one way she could think of to end this curse. Holt had to get this cabinet back to Scotland.

~

Holt pushed his chair back from the desk in the office. He was fortunate his videoconference had just ended. Caitlin stood on the desk's other side, fairly vibrating with what she was trying to tell him. He could see her lips moving and hear her voice, but the sounds she made were nonsense. Babbling. A curse carved into a cabinet. Passed down in his family. The source of all the deaths and disappearances…all the heartache…for the last couple of centuries?

"It doesn't make sense."

"Aye it does!" Caitlin objected, her accent noticeably

thickened. "Ye are no' Scottish, so ye didna grow up with this sort of thing. But I did. I've seen it."

"A nearly three-hundred-year-old curse?"

"Aye, and the ghost left behind in my cousin Ian's estate to guard family treasures just like those," she argued, pointing up toward the attic.

"Treasures?" Holt scoffed. "They don't look like treasures to me."

She started to pace from one side of the desk to the other. "No' to ye, no' nowadays, but in the eighteenth century, in a family where men were either killed at Culloden or hunted down and killed afterward for being Jacobite or having Jacobite sympathies...hell, for being Scottish? Aye. When the victors raped the women, killed their bairns, stole the clan's wealth and possessions, and carried the lot back to their estates in England? A curse would make a great deal of sense."

"That's the long, sad tale you refused to tell me at our first dinner the day I arrived? Good God, that is awful." He paused for a moment, staring aside, unable to think if he looked at her. She was incandescent in her excitement—and indignation over the history she related. But what, really, did it have to do with him? "I know I told you what my mother thought, but I don't know if I can believe this cabinet is the source— or if the curse is real."

She stopped and put her hands flat on the desk, leaning toward him. "Ye did see most of those photos. Do ye recall the ones with the sad, wee bairn or two and a single adult? Believe *them*."

He gestured for her to sit down, surprised when she

straightened, then dropped into a chair without argument. "You can't be certain when or where they were taken, or who the people are in them."

"Maybe not, but why else would they be here?" She slapped the arm of the chair, then leaned forward, elbows on knees, waving her hands as she talked. "The person who carved a curse into the very thing that likely provided income for her family did so because she knew it would be stolen. The English might have burned everything else her people owned, but they would save that cabinet. At the time, it was probably full of valuable herbs and compounds used by a healer. Things that could have helped wounded clansmen recover. Things the English would have wanted to deny the Scots. And to use for their own wounded."

"That seems reasonable." Holt hated to admit it, but what she found in the cabinet was the first tangible connection to the curse his mother had believed to be real. Maybe not proof, but it made him think.

"In Scotland, healers were often wise women— women with special sight or intuition, and training in herbs, potions, portents— passed from mother to daughter. So that curse she carved into what was likely the healer's most prized possession had teeth. And still does, as recently as your parents' generation. If I were ye, I'd take it very seriously, and I'd fly that cabinet back to the Highlands as fast as I could get it loaded on a plane."

That seemed extreme, but he wasn't about to say that out loud. "It's really got you spooked." He couldn't doubt she believed every word she was saying. What if she was right?

Caitlin sat back and crossed her arms. "If he's still alive, would you ever want to meet your father?"

The whiplash change of subject floored Holt. "Why? He hasn't bothered to be part of my life."

"How could he if he doesn't know you exist?"

That stopped Holt cold for a long minute. Then he shook his head. It didn't matter. He had no idea who his father was. His mother said he'd died, and with his mother and great-aunt dead, the family who might have known his father's name were out of reach. "If he was alive, why would I disturb the life he's lived without me. He might have another family—"

"Aye, ye might have brothers and sisters and cousins and more. Wouldn't that be wonderful?"

"Would it? How would I know?" Christ, she'd pressed her lips into a thin, taut line. An uncomfortable feeling flooded Holt's belly. Guilt for upsetting Caitlin? "Look, this is all too new— and weird. Can we leave it be for a while? You have other pieces and the catalog to finish. You said you wanted to get home before Hogmanay. Let's not get tied into knots over one cabinet."

She sighed, then stiffened. "Fine. But in the meantime, you should make arrangements to send it back."

"Send it back where?"

"To the Highlands."

"Where in the Highlands?" Holt snorted. "Put it on a truck, find a likely spot, and dump it beside the road? Advertise it and find a buyer? What?"

"I...I'll look into it. Jacobite furnishings are collectible even if they don't belong in a museum. And this one might."

"Where?"

"If we're to break this curse, Inverness, perhaps. Or an estate like my cousin's."

"Fine, see if your cousin wants it. Problem solved."

CHAPTER 9

Two mornings later, Caitlin had gotten nowhere researching the curse, and Holt had made himself scarce. Working, he told her and waved her away if she happened to catch him on his laptop in the office.

This morning, Caitlin was happy for the diversion of a trip into the village on an errand for Mrs. Smith. Before going to the market, she dropped by the bakery to get pastries and two coffees. As Alice boxed up two luscious chocolate croissants, she told the baker where she was headed. "I still haven't paid my debt, but I have a good feeling that today is the day to catch Doc Coates for a few minutes."

"Good luck. I hope he enjoys these. If he does, tell him to come by sometime for more. My treat." She winked.

Caitlin laughed and promised to deliver the message.

When she arrived at the vet's office, the reception area was full of anxious pet parents waiting for an appointment or dropping off their fur-babies. Caitlin explained her errand to the receptionist, Rachel, who took her back to the Doc's office without delay.

He stood when she entered, but she waved him back to his seat. He looked knackered.

"Ye are a hard man to catch sitting still," she told him after Rachel left them. "But I always pay my debts. I promised ye coffee, and since there's been a delay, I've added interest in the form of a treat from Alice's shop around the corner. I hope ye like chocolate."

He gave her a tired smile. "Who doesn't? This wasn't necessary, but thank you. The coffee is welcome. I've was up half the night with a horse...well, I doubt you want to hear the details."

Caitlin held up a hand. "I won't take up any more of your time, then. Your waiting area is full."

"No rush," Doc said. "My techs will let me know when they need me. I appreciate you giving me an excuse to take a few minutes to revive." He pulled a croissant out of the bag, bit into it, and smiled. "You're a lifesaver. This is great. The bakery is around the corner?"

"Alice Nash's place, yes. It's so close, I don't know how you've missed it."

He shrugged. "Work." He gestured for her to take a seat in one of the two chairs opposite his desk and leaned back into his.

"How does your wife like the crazy hours you keep?"

Doc shook his head. "Not married. Never have been." He stared into his coffee cup. "Missed my chance years ago."

Caitlin found it hard to believe a good-looking man,

and a veterinarian, too, had not been deluged with offers from attractive women. "It sounds like there's a story there."

He nodded. "A sad one."

"I'm sorry." She needed to change the subject. She came here to pay a debt, not make him miserable. "Tell me, then, how did you find yourself in Scotland?"

"It was a few years ago." He took a gulp of coffee and leaned back in his chair. "I was still in the Army." He glanced from Caitlin to the second coffee.

His meaning was clear. He wasn't in a hurry. Caitlin picked it up and settled in to listen.

"You take the other croissant, too." He favored her with a grin then continued, "I did some training with mountain rescue teams in your Munros."

"So ye ken what we call our higher hills." Caitlin bit into the second croissant and let the chocolate flow happily over her tongue.

"Over three thousand feet, yes. You have more than two hundred of them, so there's ample opportunity for people intent on bagging another Munro to get into trouble, especially as fast as the weather can change up there."

When she finished chewing, she asked, "How many did you bag?"

"Only a dozen or so. We spent most of the time on Ben Lomond and Ben Nevis, working with dogs to track lost hikers."

"That sounds exciting. Do you miss it?"

"Not the word I'd use. Gratifying. Sometimes tragic. Deceptively dangerous. But yes, I miss it. You know, I'm still doing some search-and-rescue training here. Someday I hope to open a full-scale canine training center."

"So you weren't there to train *with* them…"

He nodded and finished chewing the last bit of his croissant. "I trained them to work with dogs I also trained. Their dogs."

"Which were easier to train? The men or the dogs?"

He burst into laughter just as the receptionist, Rachel, leaned in the door.

"Sorry to interrupt, but you're needed in Treatment Two."

Caitlin dropped her unfinished croissant into the bakery bag and tucked it in her purse. "Thanks for taking a few minutes with me. I'd love to hear more, but I'll get out of your way."

"Stay here and finish yours." He moved around the desk and paused by the door. "Thanks for the coffee and chocolate. I appreciated the break."

She'd have to tell Alice he wasn't unsocial at all, just busy, and he had some interesting stories to tell. Maybe Alice should waylay him the next time she saw him. Caitlin smiled at the thought of playing matchmaker for the two of them. Alice might be just the woman the never-married, chocolate-loving Doc needed.

She sipped her coffee and fished her croissant out of the bag, then took a bite while she looked around the office. As much as she liked Holt Ridley, as much as she wanted to end his family's curse and see him happy, if she was going to make it home for Hogmanay, she was leaving here in another week. Not a lot of time to play Santa's helper. Not and finish the job she'd been hired to do.

Rachel popped back into the office. "Want to see some new puppies?"

"Aye, of course." Caitlin swallowed the last of her coffee.

"We've got five, and they're beyond adorable. Come on." With a wave, Rachel led her to the back where animals were boarded while their owners were away. Off in a quiet corner, a box guarded by the mother dog held squealing pups.

"She's been out," a vet tech told Rachel before he led another leashed dog out the back door.

Caitlin couldn't resist the puppies. "Oh, how cute!" She bent down to pet the mother while telling her softly that she wouldn't bother her babies, just look at them. She glanced around at her friend. "How do you not pick them all up and squeeze them?"

Rachel grinned. "I have to admit sometimes I do. When Mama, there, is outside taking a break. She's just back from one, or she'd be in the box with them. Oh look! She's going to feed them." Sure enough, while Caitlin's attention was on Rachel, the mother dog had hopped into the box and stretched out by her pups. One by one, squealing, noses twitching, they made their way to her and suckled.

Caitlin squatted and stared to her heart's content at little pink noses, tips of tongues that peeked out, then disappeared, tightly closed eyes, and big round puppy bellies. "I could watch them for hours. I wish I could take them all back to Scotland with me, but they wouldn't be old enough by the time I leave in a fortnight— and then there's that pesky long quarantine."

"A fortnight?"

"Ah, sorry. Two weeks, give or take."

Rachel's dismay was plain in her tone and furrowed brow. "So soon?"

She pushed to her feet. "I might have gone sooner, but Holt talked me into staying to see an American Christmas. But after that, I want to get home in time for Hogmanay— New Year's to you." And since she'd convinced Holt to fly the cabinet to her cousin Ian, she was eager to see it in its home. Not that there would be any way to tell if it lifted the curse. Only time would reveal that.

"Are you going to miss Christmas with your family?"

Caitlin pictured Ian's new family and smiled. "They'll manage quite well without me. Besides, Hogmanay is a bigger party in Scotland, and I'll be home for that."

"We'll miss you, you know."

"I'll miss all of you, too. At least we can stay in touch online. You can send me pictures of these wee bairns."

"I thought I heard voices back here," Doc Coates said as he entered the room. "Ah, the puppies. Cute, aren't they?" He leaned over the box, giving the mother a quick inspection, then each of the puppies.

"You know they are."

The bell over the front door chimed, and Rachel left them to take care of their next customer.

"Can I ask you a question?" She didn't know what he would say, but if she was delicate, he might answer. Her conversation with Mrs. Smith about Holt's missing father gave her an idea she would pass on to Holt. Surely some of the other older residents in the area might remember him and recall his mother's boyfriend's name. If Holt found more of his old friends, he might learn something. Caitlin was about to exhaust her supply of acquaintances in town. Alice was no help. She'd moved to the area only a few years ago. But Doc Coates used to live here and seemed to be the right age to have known Holt's mother. Maybe he could tell her something.

"You just asked one." He grinned.

"Besides that." Caitlin waved a hand. Her suspicion might be totally unfounded, but now that she thought about his history in town, she had a feeling about Doc Coates. It might be the daftest idea she'd had yet. But was his grin not quite Holt's, but not completely different? "You said you lived here for a short time before you went into the service and had your career. You must have traveled all over the world. Why did you come back?"

His expression turned pensive. "None of the places I'd been stationed appealed to me after I retired. I was a med tech in the service but spent a lot of time with K9 units, which gave me a head start on vet school. So I did that, then started looking for a place to settle. I liked this area, or maybe just the girlfriend I left behind."

He looked uncomfortable enough to make Caitlin wonder if he'd left behind the love of his life. "What happened to her?"

"I came back once on leave and tried to see her. Her aunt told me she was gone. When I tried to convince her to tell me where Jenny was, the aunt claimed she'd died, then closed the door in my face without telling me what happened to her."

Jenny? Her *aunt*? Caitlin's pulse leapt, then slowed as she pictured a younger Jim Coates facing the door that had just been slammed in his face. "I'm so sorry."

"It was a long time ago. Anyway, none of our school friends knew anything. If something had happened to Jenny Cooper, they should have known. Something bad would have made the papers. She just disappeared, and my leave was up. I left town and never looked back until the village vet retired at the right time for me to step in and take over the practice."

Jenny's last name was not Ridley, but there was an aunt, just like Holt's mother had an aunt in her life. Caitlin didn't want to seem too eager to find out about his past love life, so she asked, instead, "How did you find out about this job?"

"Online, like everything else these days. I checked the local paper's web edition every now and again. Always hoped I'd see some mention of what happened to Jenny. I happened to see an article about the vet's impending retirement and got in touch. Coming back permanently was a tough decision. A lot of memories here, not all good."

"But you came anyway."

"I always wondered what would have happened if I'd stayed in town. For a couple of years, even after what the aunt told me, I tried to find Jenny, but couldn't, and eventually gave up. She was the one that got away."

Without being obvious, she tried to study Jim Coates with Holt in mind while he talked. She thought there might be a resemblance, but her memory, or her sudden wishful thinking for a Christmas miracle and a joyful father-son reunion, were probably playing tricks on her.

Could it be? She turned to regard the puppies as she smoothed a damp hand over her pants leg. What if at some point Jenny's name changed from Cooper to her aunt's, Ridley, perhaps as a shot at the aunt who tossed her out on the street? Or if the aunt, as guardian, had done it before the pregnancy became known. If Jenny did move away, but to a nearby village, as a single mother, she probably would not have stayed in touch with the same circles Jim Coates knew her to frequent from high school. And if she was Holt's mother, what a shame Doc Coates hadn't found her — and his son— before she died for real.

Coates moved to the box and squatted next to Caitlin, studying the puppies as they nursed. He reached out to pet the mother before pushing to his feet. "I always hoped her aunt had lied and Jenny married, changed her name, and moved somewhere with someone who made her happy."

His empathy for the animals in his care was obvious to Caitlin. His wish for his old girlfriend reinforced her good impression of him. But how would he react if he found out what Caitlin hoped was the truth? He'd said Jenny was the one that got away. Would he be open to the possibility that he had a grown son by the woman who was the love of his life? And who could tell him? Caitlin didn't think it was her place to break news like that, but so far, she was the only one who might know the rest of Jenny's story.

She needed a good picture of him. Or a DNA sample. Not that she would know what to do with one if she got it.

But a paternity test would confirm any relationship with scientific certainty. In the meantime, she'd just have to have faith that it would all work out. And soon.

Rachel came back in before Caitlin came up with a response.

"Did you tell Doc how soon you're leaving? I can't believe it." Then she perked up. "Hey, let me get a picture of the two of you, so you have that to remember us by."

Caitlin grinned. Just what she needed. "And then the doc can take one of you and me," she added to be polite, and because Rachel had become a friend. But she really wanted that picture of him.

They posed using Caitlin's phone, then Caitlin made her excuses and left, prized photo safely in her possession.

~

Caitlin spent the next several hours studying the photo Rachel had taken of Dr. Coates, doodling on her notepad, then writing more names, drawing connecting lines, and getting nowhere. Could he be the father missing from Holt's life? She just couldn't be sure. About him, or about the picture of Mrs. Smith's son in the kitchen. Deciding she wanted another look at it, she clipped her notepad under the photo of the carved curse and tucked them under a pile of paperwork. Then she got up and headed for the kitchen, intent on drowning her frustration with Holt's family history in something deliciously diverting. "Mrs. Smith, any chance you have any of your special hot chocolate ready? I could use some about now."

The housekeeper gave her a kind smile. "Sure, dear. Have a seat, and I'll warm it for you. What's wrong?"

Caitlin dropped into a chair at the kitchen table. "Nothing, really. And everything. I've found some things that may be important to Holt's family history but aren't actually proof of anything."

Mrs. Smith poured from a pitcher in the fridge into a large mug, popped it in the microwave and tapped a few buttons. Its whir started up, and in moments, a comforting, rich scent of chocolate and spices filled the air.

Caitlin inhaled and felt the tension ooze from her shoulders. "That recipe of yours is pure magic," she said. "Just the scent makes me feel better."

"Christmas magic does that, you know."

"I didn't, until now. You might send a mug of this to Holt. I suspect he could use some Christmas magic right about now, too. He doesn't want to believe in the Scottish kind."

"Perhaps later. I believe he went with Farrell to the garages to inspect the antique autos. His great-aunt kept her husband's collection, though I've no idea why. She never drove them." Mrs. Smith turned at the beep and took a steaming mug from the microwave. "Now, what do you mean by *he doesn't believe in the Scottish kind?*" She set the chocolate in front of Caitlin. "Let that be for a minute or you'll scald your tongue."

Caitlin nodded. "I found evidence in a piece of furniture in the attic that may have something to do with why Holt's family has such a sad history."

Mrs. Smith's eyebrows lifted to her hairline. "What kind of evidence?"

"If I'm right, a curse made by a Scottish healer, a wise woman, who lost her love to the English, either during Culloden, a battle that led to the destruction of the Highland way of life in the mid-1700s, or soon after. That sort of curse can be powerful."

"Oh, dear." Mrs. Smith leaned back against the sink apron and crossed her arms. Her tone didn't convey incredulity or sympathy. Just…resignation?

Caitlin leaned forward and rested her chin on her fist. "You don't seem surprised."

"I've taken care of this family for many years. I knew Holt's great-aunt's father, though I was just a young girl. No mother, I'm sorry to say. She died young. The lack soured Amelia as a child, and she grew even more sour the older she got. As did the loss of her husband a few years after they married, before they could be blessed with children. I think she knew something wasn't right."

So the curse had followed the great-aunt's line, not Holt's great-uncle's? Then jumped to his brother, Holt's grandfather, when the great-aunt had no children? And no other direct relations? How many times down through the years had that happened? And how distant from Holt and his mother was the relative who had originally owned— and cursed— the apothecary cabinet? Holt might never agree, but Caitlin would love to hire a genealogist to trace the family connections back to 1746. "You knew Holt's mother. She lived here for a while."

"Of course. She and my son were friends." She glanced around at the picture she kept on the windowsill and studied it for a moment, then turned back to Caitlin. "And I met that boy she was seeing one time before...well, he went off. Joined the military, I heard. Probably killed somewhere far away."

Caitlin's heart sank. For Mrs. Smith's loss, and for Holt's. She'd been so set on helping Holt reunite with the father he'd never known, she hadn't considered that he might really be dead. "Do you remember his name?"

"Hmmm. I haven't thought about him in decades. Johnny? Jimmy. Maybe Gene? Something with a 'J' sound."

"What about his last name?"

Mrs. Smith shook her head. "If I ever knew it, it's long gone. And what does it matter? Holt has his mother's name. Her aunt's inheritance, though that's small compensation for the way she treated that girl. End of story."

Caitlin sipped her hot chocolate quietly for several minutes while Mrs. Smith bustled around the kitchen, then excused herself. Caitlin remained, inhaling the comforting scent of the dregs of her cocoa. She needed to talk to Holt. He'd never actually told her his mother's first name, or whether she'd ever gone by a last name other than the one she'd given to him. Doc Coates's story ran too closely parallel to the little Holt knew about his origins for her to be wrong in questioning his past. If they weren't father and son, they were part of the biggest coincidence she'd ever seen.

After Mrs. Smith left, Caitlin considered what the housekeeper thought she knew about Holt's father and her supposition that he had died in the military. Calling up her picture of Doc Coates on her phone, she held it up so she could see the photo on the windowsill at the same time. She studied both to fix their features in her mind and muttered, "Maybe. Maybe not." Unable to come up with an answer, she headed for the attic to see what other mysteries she might unearth. She'd talk to Holt later.

~

Looking at antique cars got Holt thinking about what else his family had held onto down through the ages. He'd had been doing some reading about the 18th Century Jacobite rising, not that he'd tell Caitlin her theories had intrigued him. He was appalled by the violence against the Scottish people following Culloden in 1745. What he read lent credence to Caitlin's assertion that because of a love lost in that epic battle or its aftermath, someone might carve a curse into an apothecary cabinet they expected to be stolen. Whether a curse could be real or have any real effect was debatable. But the more he read and the more he recalled those sad, empty eyes in the photos in the trunk, the more he entertained the possibility his mother had been telling the literal truth.

He decided he wanted another look at Caitlin's photos of the carving and her notes. She'd gone into town earlier, but he knew she had printed out the composite she'd created. If he could find that, he wouldn't have to invade her privacy by searching for it on her laptop, something, after working side-by-side with her, he knew he could do with no technical impediment. He grimaced. Who didn't password-protect their computers? Caitlin must either be very trusting or from an area where crime, especially cybercrime, was non-existent. He went up to the attic first, thinking she'd left all her research with the cabinet where she'd been working. He didn't find anything there, so he came downstairs to the office.

The table Caitlin used looked a mess. She'd piled papers and print-outs of pictures of items in the house haphazardly at the corners then filled the middle with random lists, scraps of notes, and who knew what.

Holt went around to her chair, surveyed the mess, and realized she had a system. He'd find what he wanted in one of the piles since, based on what he saw on top of each of them, they seemed to be stacks that contained more detailed information about specific items of furniture. He thumbed through the first, careful not to disturb the order in which she'd placed things. He hated when his assistant tried to find something on his desk, or worse, took it into her head to organize the papers on it. He didn't want to be guilty of doing the same to Caitlin.

Not finding what he wanted, he moved to another corner, but something in the middle of the table caught his eye— the glossy edge of a photo. Mostly covered by another sheet that contained a to-do list, a bit of rough wood and two letters of the carved inscription were visible.

Holt picked up the list, intending to study the photo

beneath it, but couldn't resist the chance to see what Caitlin had left to do before she returned to Scotland. He chuckled at some of the things she listed, including gift ideas for her family in Scotland, then noticed his name on her shopping list.

He sank into the chair behind him. She was going to give him a Christmas present? She didn't need to do that. Worse, it meant he needed to shop for something for her but had no idea what she'd like. And what about Farrell and Mrs. Smith? He'd been so focused on finishing the work here and returning to California, he had forgotten all about the holiday. As the new owner, he would be expected to provide some sort of holiday bonus or gifts, wouldn't he?

He should talk to Mrs. Smith and find out what she'd told Caitlin about his family history. That might give him a chance to find out what she and Farrell had received from his great-aunt in the past for the holidays. If not, he'd bet Caitlin already knew. Not that he wanted her to think taking care of the help was an afterthought. But she would understand his focus being on the estate, its contents, and the mystery she'd uncovered rather than on Santa, peppermint sticks, and gaily wrapped packages. Somehow, the two did not go well together.

He made a mental note to call the lawyer and see if his great-aunt had left any instructions about holiday gifts and bonuses for the staff or, more importantly, if she had provided for their retirement in the event he sold the estate. He should have questioned that much earlier and suspected some of Caitlin's glowing comments about them had been intended to make him recall his responsibilities to them. For a change, she'd been too subtle. For the immediate issue of the holiday, if all else failed, he could just ask them what their employer used to do for them, but he disliked putting them on the spot and worse, making them feel they had been overlooked. He was usually better with people than that.

While he castigated himself, he set aside the to-do list and noticed a paperclip on the picture of the carved inscription. He picked up the packet to see what Caitlin had clipped with it. Several scraps of random-looking notes about the family curse, a rough genealogy chart going back to his great-aunt's parents that listed Mrs. Smith's name to the side, her son's underlined below it, and one other name she'd underlined several times along the margin. Both were connected to a notation saying "Holt's mother" with a plus sign. What the hell? Did the veterinarian have something to do with his family history? His mother? Had Mrs. Smith told her things about his family that Holt was not privy to? About her son and his mother? Caitlin had asked him if he wanted to find his father. Then, he hadn't been sure if he did, but Caitlin clearly hadn't dropped the idea.

He slapped the packet down on the desk, shifting the top items in the corner piles with the breeze he created. He stood and straightened them, then checked the floor around the desk to make sure nothing had flown off. While he did that, he thought about why he'd come east. He'd wanted to cut all ties as quickly as possible, so he hadn't inquired about his mother, her friends, or anything else that would have created more connections to this place. Was he ignoring an opportunity? Though he'd asked her to stay out of his personal life, perhaps Caitlin had been asking the questions he should have been. Not just focusing on his mother's past but trying harder to find out about his father.

He picked up the packet again and flipped through it. The last page floored him. A list of local labs doing DNA testing. What was she up to? In order to have something to test, she had to have someone in mind to test. Mrs. Smith? Doc Coates? The way Caitlin underlined his name, she must think him important. Holt pictured the veterinarian. Could they be related? Holt didn't see a strong resemblance, and certainly not one that would imply a father/son relationship. So why had Caitlin connected the vet's name with a note about Holt's mother? And underlined his name several times?

At a loss, Holt set the to-do list aside and studied the composite photo. Weren't curses usually pronounced in Latin? Or had he been watching too many movies? He didn't speak more than enough French to order a bottle of Beaujolais and ask for directions to the men's room, so he couldn't say whether the language in the carving was consistent with what was spoken in the 18th century or a more modern attempt at a hoax. Clearly, he wasn't going to glean any insights from the photo other than those he and Caitlin had already discussed.

Frustrated, he replaced the photo packet under the to-do list and sat back. He'd come in here to look into one mystery and found another. What did a genealogy chart, a list of DNA testing labs and several notations of names have in common with a photo of a presumed ancient French curse in a piece of 18th century Scottish furniture? Besides being evidence that Caitlin was delving into his family history? He clenched his jaw, uncomfortable despite knowing he'd set her on this path. Still, she was taking it much further than he'd expected. He didn't know what to do about any of it. There were no hard-and-fast answers to be found in ancient family history. They didn't have enough information, and historical records from the time period of the carved curse were, as far as Holt's brief foray into research let him suppose, sketchy at best.

That left his meddling appraiser. The simplest way to an explanation of what Caitlin was up to with her underlined names and list of labs would be to ask her. And then she'd know he'd been snooping on her desk. She'd probably be pissed. Or maybe not. Maybe she'd be pleased that he was taking enough of an interest in his background and family history to look through her research and question what she was doing. He snorted out a laugh. Sure, she would.

CHAPTER 10

After two fruitless hours in the attic, Caitlin discovered little more than dusty, but modern, broken furniture. She had a look in some of the boxes she'd ignored earlier and discovered twentieth-century Christmas cards someone had saved. They might provide more leads to check into. Anyone close enough to the family to exchange cards might be able to provide more answers. But not now. Giving up, she went in search of Holt. She found him where she expected, in the office where they'd first met. He was reading and didn't seem to notice her presence in the doorway, so she leaned on the jamb and studied him, noting the similarities with either of the men she believed could be his father. The nose and chin were similar in all. The eye and hair color were different. Holt was a little taller than Doc Coates but had the same long-limbed build. If her wild theory was right, she could see him in Holt, though suspected Holt took after his mother more than his father. She couldn't be certain based on looks alone, but add their histories to the mix, and it made sense.

She must have made a noise because he glanced up and noticed her.

"Caitlin, do you need something?"

In for a penny… "What was your mother's name?"

"Her name? Why do you want to know that?"

"Humor me. I'll tell you in a minute."

"Jennifer Ridley."

Caitlin's heart dropped. "Jennifer Cooper Ridley?"

"How did you know that?"

Her heart started pounding a staccato beat in her chest. She grabbed onto the doorjamb to stay upright, kicking herself for not being prepared for a confirming answer, and took a deep breath. She had to get through this without hurting Holt any more than he'd already been hurt. "I learned it from the man who might be your father."

Holt frowned and leaned back in his chair. "He's here? Who is he?"

"I…I can't say."

"Can't? Or won't?"

She held up a hand to forestall his questions. "I don't have permission…"

"What does that mean?" Holt straightened up. His brows drew together.

"It means he doesn't know about you, either. He told me he had a girlfriend in school named Jenny Cooper."

After a dismissive wave, Holt said, "There might have

been more than one Jenny Cooper. Maybe Ginny with a G-I, not J-E. And even if he meant my mother, a lot of people went to school with her. She probably had plenty of friends, even boyfriends. What's so special about this one?"

Caitlin crossed the room to Holt's desk and perched on the edge near him. He was looking as dazed by her announcement as she felt. Without mentioning his name, she repeated what Doc Coates told her about his military career and the timing of his return on leave to the village years ago, leaving out vet school. Mentioning it would be a dead giveaway. "He thinks your mother married, changed her name, and moved away. He has no idea you exist."

Holt leaned away so suddenly, the chair tipped.

Caitlin grabbed the arm to keep him from going over. "If I squint, you look like him, but not a lot. You must have taken after your mother. A simple paternity test would prove whether it's true."

"DNA. Right. I saw the list of labs on your desk. The genealogy chart you drew."

He knew! "You went through my desk?" He'd let her rattle on when the whole time, he knew who she meant. Caitlin swallowed against the sudden burn at the back of her throat.

"You're going through my life," Holt reminded her.

"Not the same."

"No, it's not. What you're doing is…more. You have plenty of access to things I've touched. You could easily take something with my DNA on it. Hell, you don't even need to go to that trouble. All you and Doc Coates have to do is fake a report."

Even though she'd been warned, she flinched when he said Doc Coates's name. "I would never do anything like that. Nor would he. He's a good man." Caitlin clenched her fists. How could he think she'd try to hurt him like this? "I know this is a shock, but I've told you the truth, and as much as I know." Not quite, she'd withheld the veterinary training, but Holt knew that, too.

Suddenly the skin around Holt's mouth turned white, and a muscle in his jaw flexed. "If this is a scam to get access to my money…" He trailed off and shook his head. "I can't believe you'd be party to such a thing."

Caitlin froze, her stomach sinking. She expected him to be dubious about finding his father, but suspicious of her? Why? Anger made her blood heat, and she fought to keep her voice calm.

"I am not a party to anything. No one is trying to steal from you." She took a breath and stood. "I told you what… Doc Coates…told me about his past. We were just having a conversation. He was answering my questions, not trying to convince me of some elaborate, fraudulent scheme."

Holt's immediate reaction to think she was a con artist hurt and scared her. She struggled not to let that show, keeping her voice even and her expression bland. She had hoped finding his father would be over-the-top good news for him. Now she wondered if she'd wildly overstepped her bounds. "He's not claiming any connection with you. I'm the one who thinks there may be one, and I thought you'd want to know."

Holt frowned. "I know better than most how appearances can be deceiving. And the very people who are supposed to love and take care of you can turn on you in a heartbeat. An infant's heartbeat, at that. Besides, you forget, my mother said my father died."

"She might have thought so," Caitlin replied, "or just said that because she didn't know what happened to him. Or maybe that's what her aunt told her. Maybe she didn't want you to keep asking about him. If he went away…"

"Oh, he did that," Holt bit out. "One way or the other."

Caitlin stood and moved to the other side of the desk, needing some distance between them. It wasn't fair that Holt and his mother had been treated so badly. Caitlin knew that. But she was not his great-aunt. And she was not trying to rip him off. "If I have the timing right, he left before your mother knew about you. He didn't know he was leaving you, and I don't know why he felt he had to leave her. But based on what I've seen of Doc Coates, he must have had a good reason."

"Neither of us knows him. I've met him once, and you have spent, what, an hour with him in total? Two? That doesn't make you an expert on him— or who we was in high school. Nor, despite what you've done here since you arrived, are you an expert on me and my family."

"I care about you," she insisted, hearing the bubbling anger in his voice. This was not the reaction she'd wanted to her news. She reached out a hand, then dropped it when his gaze shifted away. "I do care about you. Once you get over this shock, you'll remember that and stop throwing around crazy accusations."

Holt shook his head. "People have tried to scam me before. I spent the last six months in court because of a woman who got close to me and tried to steal my company's secrets." He stared off into space for a long moment. "I can't let you be another."

Caitlin held her breath, afraid to move. He was working himself up, and it was her fault. "Holt, if you don't want to know if he's your father, or anything else, then *dinna fash*. I'll forget all of it. I thought I was helping you, but I see now I was wrong. Your past, your family, is none of my business. I'll finish the catalog and be on my way back to Scotland and out of your life before ye ken it."

Holt nodded, but something in his gaze reflected pain. Caitlin did not want to imagine its depth. He'd been abandoned by his father and his great-aunt before he was born. His mother's early death was another abandonment. Then some woman at work betrayed him. Given that series of events, she could understand why he had no reason to trust another woman. To trust her. Except she'd told the truth when she said she cared about him. They'd grown close during their time together. He couldn't deny that. He had feelings for her, she was sure of it, just as she had for him.

Then he grimaced and looked away. "Maybe it's best if you leave now," he finally said. "You want to be with your family for New Year's. You can be there for Christmas, too."

"What?" She could not have heard him correctly. Her belly filled with ice. "Go home? I haven't finished my work here."

She cared about Holt and believed he would remember he cared about her, if only he'd calm down. He must! She'd been a fool to think he would go along with her efforts to find his father. How could she have been so wrong? She should have known he'd have deeply buried pain. Instead, she'd clawed her way into wherever he'd kept it hidden and ripped away the indifference he used to keep it buried. And she'd done it here in this house he hated. Here, where he'd seen his mother subjected to misery and unspoken pain by the one person who was supposed to take care of her.

Caitlin realized she had made the man seem real who was the cause of all of that happened to his mother and to him. She'd effectively called his mother a liar by introducing the possibility that she had lied about his father's death. Add that to all the horror the discovery of his family's legacy in the attic had shown him, and she had been the one to bring it to light after it had been hidden away for decades.

"I only wanted to help bring you some happiness," she told him, her voice low and gravelly. "Instead, I've ruined everything."

"No, you haven't." He sighed, giving her a moment of hope, but he still didn't look at her. "Maybe we need to turn down the heat for a while. Drop all of this and just think. I'm stuck here for the winter, but you're not."

Nay! This couldn't be happening.

"You can finish the catalog anywhere," Holt continued, his voice a sickening monotone. "I'll fly you home for the holidays on my jet. I can have it here in the morning. You can take that damn apothecary cabinet with you when you go."

"But…what if I need to come back?" *What if you want me to come back?* She couldn't ask the question. Losing Holt was bad enough. Losing Holt under a cloud of suspicion? The blows coming one after the other nearly doubled her over. Her professional reputation and dreams of the perfect job fizzled in front of her eyes along with any belief that Holt cared for her. In his eyes, she was just another woman out to get him— or to get from him anything she could.

"We'll deal with that after the first of the year. After you take a break and have a chance to look through what you've collected so far." He turned his gaze on her, as cold and gray as the winter sky. "You'd better go pack."

Holt looked miserable but resolute. He still wouldn't meet her gaze, and that scared her. He'd talked himself into this. He meant it. Defeated, Caitlin left Holt alone.

What could she do? She had no choice but to do as he asked— and go.

~

The next morning, Holt was focused on clearing his email queue and keeping his mind off a certain Scottish lass when the office door opened. He didn't look up from his laptop. "Yes, Farrell?" A boom of thunder rattled the windows, followed by a long, low rumble. Perfect. Just the weather to reinforce his rotten mood.

A higher voice than he expected answered, "It's me, Holt."

Caitlin. He kept his gaze on the screen in front of him, hoping if he ignored her, she'd go away. With that scheme to make him think she'd found his father, she'd opened old wounds yesterday, and ripped wider the wound he'd exposed in the damned gazebo. Hell, he'd even agreed to sending the apothecary cabinet to her cousin in the Highlands. Was she trying to take the most valuable piece for herself? He'd made it damned easy for her to scam him, complete with a convenient family curse she could use to make him want to get rid of it. Had she somehow faked the inscription, or just faked the image of it? He could clear that up himself by using his phone in the cabinet the same way she had. Okay, possibly one point in her favor.

But he'd let himself trust her when he should have known better. He'd been fooled before by a woman who professed to care about him. He'd be a damned idiot to let it happen again.

Yet he'd trusted Caitlin. He'd fallen fast for her. And if he took a breath and thought back over the time they'd had together, the discoveries they'd shared, he couldn't stay angry with her. Disappointed, if his suspicions were correct. But now that he'd slept on it, he knew he had no real evidence. The curse would be hard to prove or disprove, but what did he care about one old cabinet? And DNA samples sent to a lab of his choice would provide irrefutable proof of her sincerity, and, possibly, his father's. His reaction yesterday was all about his painful history— a history that had nothing to do with her.

Caitlin cleared her throat, pulling him from his spiral of disappointment and anger.

"Mrs. Smith asked me to pry you out of here, or I wouldn't disturb you. She's making pancakes."

Caitlin's frown told him she was still angry. She had reason to be.

It was his fault. Holt met her gaze, trying to read her, to see into her soul. He wanted to trust her again. Despite the obvious irritation in her voice, he should be glad she was still there, not on her way to Islip to board his jet. She didn't look happy to be confronting him— her shoulders were nearly up to her ears, and the knuckles of the hand gripping the doorjamb were white.

He intended to ask her to come sit with him and let him apologize when she pointed at the ceiling.

"I imagine by now your pilot has probably informed you this weather isn't good for flying."

Just then, his laptop emitted a ping. Holt checked, then nodded. "Just now, actually. He got the local forecast late last night and stayed in California. This front stretches all the way to the Gulf." She couldn't go home until he— and the weather, he thought as another loud crash of thunder sounded— let her go. He might have a chance to salvage whatever had begun to grow between them. He could start by not being the horse's ass he was yesterday. "I'm glad he did. I wouldn't want you to risk flying anywhere in this storm." *Or anywhere at all away from me.* But he dared not say the words. Not yet. Not until he had a few answers. And a better gauge on her mood. He rubbed a hand over his face and finally met her gaze.

Something sparked in her eyes, making Holt's belly clench with an unfamiliar sensation. Hope. He tried to quash the feeling, but it persisted, rocking him. He couldn't have the conversation with her that he wanted until he regained his equilibrium.

Standing, Holt hooked a thumb toward the kitchen. "As long as you're stuck here, we might as well eat." He meant it as an olive branch if merely a broken one.

She leaned further into the room and crossed her arms. "The delay gives me time to work on the catalog you'll need to dispose of everything." She paused a beat and added, "Should I include my photo in it, too?"

She'd grabbed his virtual broken olive branch and jerked it right out of his virtual hand.

Holt snorted and moved toward her, but she held her ground. So much for making amends using food. He'd been too subtle. He stopped and counted to three. He had to stay calm, or she'd bolt. "Look, now that I've slept on it, I'm sorry I reacted so harshly. As I said, I've been burned before by women I cared about and thought cared about me. So that attitude I tossed at you has become a knee-jerk reaction. After the way this week has gone, I don't— I didn't know what, or who, to believe. I'm sorry I acted like an ass. You have a right to be mad at me. But I hope you'll forgive me. And I do need that catalog."

"So, you'll play nice in order to get it?"

He deserved that. He did, but it irritated him all the same. "I'm trying to apologize, damn it. Don't push your luck." He moved to brush past her.

Caitlin grasped his forearm and stopped him. "It's not mine in question. Yours is the only luck— and future— at risk."

"I...wish we had proof."

"I offered a way to get it…and you bit my head off." Caitlin waved an open hand in front of her face, forestalling any reply. "Fine. Never mind. I smell bacon. And coffee. That takes precedence over arguing with you." She stalked down the hall and didn't look around to see if he followed.

"Ah, just in time," Mrs. Smith announced as Caitlin entered the kitchen, Holt on her heels. "And Mr. Ridley, too." She added pancakes to the steaming stack on a serving platter and poured more batter onto the griddle. "Coffee?"

"Yes," Holt answered.

"And breakfast?" Mrs. Smith poured coffee into a mug and handed it to him.

Holt nodded and found a seat at the table next to Farrell, who nodded a greeting. He inhaled the scent of bacon, pancakes on the griddle, melting butter and maple syrup, letting them calm him. The kitchen never seemed so cozy to him as it did right now. Much more than when he first arrived from California, or, he supposed, as it might have been if he'd been in it as a child.

Caitlin moved toward the table, then paused, her gaze on Mrs. Smith. "Can I help?" She gestured toward the massive refrigerator/freezer pair that took up most of one wall in the kitchen. "I can pour the orange juice."

So that's the way she wanted to play it? She couldn't sit with him for a few minutes before breakfast was ready—she'd rather ignore him. Or was she simply doing her best to avoid another argument? Holt straightened and reached for his coffee, at a loss for anything to say to Farrell or Mrs.

Smith or Caitlin. Yet he didn't want to let Caitlin think he wanted to ignore her, either.

"Thank you, dear." Mrs. Smith flipped the last set of pancakes while Caitlin poured juice for the four of them and then set the glasses at each place setting on the table. She added the pitcher, too, before taking a seat beside Holt.

A long rumble of thunder rattled dishes. The lights flickered but stayed on.

"*Dreich* weather we're having," Caitlin muttered.

"Don't worry, dear," Mrs. Smith told her as Farrell stood and took the platter of pancakes and bacon from her and set it on the table. "Storms usually blow through quickly. It should be over soon." She joined them at the table. "Do you have weather like this where you're from?"

"Occasionally." Caitlin's gaze shifted to the platter being passed around the table. When it reached her, she took a serving, then lifted it toward Holt.

Her hand brushed his, and scattered hot prickles ran up his arm and down through his torso to his groin. He forced himself to ignore the sensation and took a helping of breakfast without meeting her gaze.

Then the lights went out.

"Well," Mrs. Smith said, rising, "it's a good thing we cook and heat this place with gas. Now, where did I put those candles?" She pulled open one drawer after another. "This dreary daylight is enough to see by, but since we're sharing a meal...ah, there they are...we may as well be romantic." She lit two tapers she'd placed in holders and brought them to the table. "Now, that's better." She looked at Holt. "I remember your mother used to laugh at storms.

She was a lovely girl. Lively and brave. Had to be, after what happened."

Holt cleared his throat and bent back to his breakfast. "After what?"

"After that boy she dated disappeared. Well, it's a shame he left town so suddenly. My boy and she were friends. He was in the same class at school and knew about the arguments her boyfriend had with his father. As I told Ms. Paterson, I heard he went into the army. Never came back. I imagine he's dead." She lifted a hand to her mouth, flustered. "Oh, I'm so sorry…I didn't mean…"

Caitlin filled the embarrassed silence as Holt dropped his gaze to his plate. "Since we talked, have ye remembered his name?"

Mrs. Smith shook her head. "James, I think. Or John. My boy would have known it, of course, but he was killed in the desert years ago." She glanced at the photo on the windowsill.

"I'm so sorry," Holt choked out. He was surprised he could speak around the lump in his throat and the thrumming in his chest. Dr. Coates was Jim Coates. James. Mrs. Smith had probably just confirmed Caitlin's story. His disappointment in her evaporated like the echoes of distant thunder. But she also added another wrinkle, one he needed to think about. What should he do with this information?

"I am, too," Mrs. Smith answered, "and sorry I can't be certain of his name. Perhaps someone who lived in town then might know. One of your mother's old classmates, perhaps. Were you able to contact any of them?"

Holt shook his head. "I met one of mine, but he didn't know anything useful. He'd seen some of my mother's friends— or coworkers— but not for years. I haven't tried to find anyone else. I'm not sure where I would start." He didn't count Doc Coates. They had the doc's story— or thought they did.

Suddenly, Caitlin reared back in her chair. "I know! Most schools do a book— a yearbook, aye? And keep previous classes' editions? If we can find one of those…"

"The school Mr. Ridley's mother attended was torn down years ago," Farrell informed them.

"Maybe the local library has copies."

Caitlin's sudden enthusiasm was infectious. Holt nodded. "Worth a try." He smiled at Caitlin, feeling lighter than he had since blowing up at her yesterday. She smiled back. Then thunder rumbled, closer again and he glanced up toward the ceiling. "Tomorrow, not today."

～

The next morning, Holt tried to focus on work, staring at his laptop screen until the words displayed on it should have been burned into his brain. His ability to concentrate was one of his greatest strengths and one of the reasons his business was so successful. But he had a problem. A pretty, auburn-haired, feisty, Scottish lass of a problem. The one who insisted on working in the office at the big table, where, she said, she could spread out her notes and see everything at a glance. And the one who drew his gaze and his thoughts like a magnet. A powerful magnet. Yet she seemed to have no problem at all ignoring his presence, judging by the rustling of paper and tapping of keys on her laptop. The considerately muted sounds coming from that side of the room sounded like a symphony that...damn it...even thunder couldn't compete with her presence.

Meals, breaks. They couldn't get away from each other, thanks to the stormy weather. He suspected she knew exactly what she was doing, messing with him and paying him back for accusing her of fraud. Not that he didn't deserve serious payback. He couldn't deny he'd flown off the proverbial handle. If he'd gone along with her DNA testing idea from the beginning, the question of his paternity might be solved by now.

He glanced at Caitlin, relieved that she seemed focused on her work. He studied her, imagining what life with her could be like, what their children might look like. And wondering how many she wanted to have.

And whether being involved with him really would put her in danger from some 18th-century Scottish curse. He'd laugh it off, but for those old pictures and the sad faces, despite the holiday trappings that surrounded them. Unlike the usual stoic expressions common to early photography, when the subject had to hold a pose for an inordinate amount of time, many of these eyes reflected grief and tragedy— or so he imagined.

He'd been with her when they'd opened that chest, and from its condition, it hadn't been opened in decades. No, she hadn't faked those pictures. Or the carving in the apothecary cabinet that was the source of all their disquiet.

Caitlin had arrived only a day or two before he had. And Mrs. Smith and Farrell separately confirmed she had been unaware of the attic space, and when they'd told her about it, her reaction had been genuine surprise and excitement. There hadn't been time for her to do anything so elaborate as a hoax involving that apothecary cabinet. He'd run his fingers over the carving. Even taken a few of his own photos. It was real. And perhaps all the misery that had followed his family down through the generations really had started there.

He was used to people trying to swindle him. He'd developed his suspicious nature the hard way— by being taken advantage of by people who only had their eyes on his money or his power.

And while he didn't know either Farrell or Mrs. Smith before he arrived here, his mother had spoken fondly of Mrs. Smith, even after the gazebo incident when her aunt had banished them from ever setting foot on the property. Mrs. Smith would not be involved in any plot. He'd bet his fortune on it.

In fact, he was.

He sighed and turned his thoughts to the man Caitlin supposed might be his father. She insisted there was a resemblance, though Holt agreed with Caitlin's supposition. He had always been told he took after his mother. He was starting to look forward to proof about his father.

Did he even want a father? He'd been without one his whole life. He didn't know how to be a son to a man who'd been absent since before he was born. The thought made him angry at himself for buying into the soft-headed idea, at the man for leaving his mother, and at Caitlin for opening this whole can of worms. But damn if he didn't admire her tenacity. And creativity. He'd never thought to research his mother's past. He'd just wanted to get as far from anything to do with it and with this place as he could. That had been a mistake.

He looked at Caitlin, working away at her desk by the window, pausing to flip pages in her notes, then tap-tap-tapping some more, oblivious to the disquiet she'd created in him. He didn't know what to do about Ms. Caitlin Paterson, but despite all of it, the one thing he didn't want to do was to go back to living without her. She irritated him. Challenged him. Questioned everything about him, his very parentage included. He should want her gone. Now. Today. But he didn't. He couldn't.

It made no sense. She'd added to the confusion in his life. Confusion he didn't need amplified. His great-aunt had turned his life on its head years ago, before it was barely started, and again with her damned bequest. And then Caitlin with her curiosity and her Scottish myths and legends. His curse. Seriously? In this day and age, what was he supposed to do with that? But the carving. The stereographs. His mother's beliefs. His family history, what little he knew of it.

Caitlin thought the solution was simple. Send one old cabinet back to Scotland and *voilà*, centuries of misery would end, just like that. And he'd live happily ever after. With someone.

Sure.

But what if she was right? What if the curse was real?

Could he end it? And by doing so, could he have her and keep her safe? And keep her in his life? Talk about a Christmas miracle.

He cleared his throat, and Caitlin looked up. She smiled at him. Then her gaze returned to her work.

Holt's chest squeezed at that smile. So like her to forget she should be furious with him. For a moment, at least.

CHAPTER 11

Caitlin didn't want to, but she forgave Holt. He looked so pensive sitting at the other desk, staring at the screen but doing nothing, that she couldn't help it. She'd caught him looking at her and had no choice but to give him a polite smile, then go back to her work while the storm still raged outside.

Thinking back over their interactions since he'd arrived, she could see how their attachment had grown. She wondered if she was being irrational to let herself go warm and breathless at the sound of his voice? Or with a glance from his moody gray eyes? He was way out of her league, rich and handsome, and sadly, tortured by his family history. If he genuinely was interested in her, how would she fit into his lifestyle? His life? She didn't know. But truth be told, she would like to try. He needed someone. Not that the someone had to be her, but he needed a family of his own. He'd been without anyone since his mother's death.

She wrinkled her nose, knowing such imaginings were futile. She'd be leaving as soon as the storm broke. The rough catalog was nearly done. A few more hours to finish it, and a few more after that to make sure she polished it to its preliminary shine, and she'd have no reason to stay. She could do the rest of her research at home and finish the catalog there, then email it to Holt so he could have it printed here.

She would have no reason to stay— except the mystery of Holt's parentage. She really wanted to know if, as she suspected, he and Doc Coates were father and son. But Holt had been so angry at her suggestion that she dared not bring a paternity test up again. She'd proposed looking at the yearbooks since she didn't dare recommend he go directly to Doc Coates. Maybe he'd start to open up to the idea if he saw his mother's and Doc's pictures on the same page in their old school album. If there were a way to salvage anything out of the pain she'd caused him, that would be a place to start.

Holt's sigh brought her attention back to him.

"We need to talk," he said.

Caitlin's stomach clenched. He meant about the arrangements for her departure, no doubt. "Aye?"

"I've thought it over. You're right. I...there's no harm in doing the paternity test. DNA. Whatever. If he's my father, both of us— all of us— should know it."

Did he mean it? Caitlin's heart warmed to hear he wanted to include her in finding out. She was tempted to jump up and hug him for coming to his senses but restrained her impulse. "You pick the lab, so you're comfortable with the result. Or labs. Send samples to several..."

"No. One will do. More than that might attract attention I don't want."

"Oh, of course." She could see the headline now: *Who's Your Daddy? Billionaire Ridley Tests DNA*. He'd be mortified. Though it was likely many people knew he'd been raised by a single mother, he wouldn't want his family history dragged into the spotlight. Or worse, have people think he was challenging some woman's paternity claim for her child.

"And I'll fly the cabinet to Scotland when the storm breaks. Just tell me where to send it."

He stood and moved toward her, the look in his eyes capturing her, holding her in place, breath bottled up in her chest until he said, "But I want you to stay."

Caitlin was on her feet before she realized she'd moved. Holt met her in the middle of the office. He didn't embrace her. She didn't expect him to. Instead, he reached out and brushed her hair behind her ear. "The catalog is nearly done," she felt honor-bound to tell him. "I could go with the cabinet— if you still want to get rid of me."

"Don't make this hard on me, Caitlin. I know you're only trying to make my life better. I can't help thinking you're being overly superstitious, but we'll send the cabinet to Scotland, to a museum, or to hell. I don't care. We'll do what you think best. As long as you stay."

"I planned to be home for Hogmanay." Why was she arguing with him?

The crease between Holt's brows deepened. "If that's

what you really want— it's your decision. But I won't send you away. As soon as the weather clears, the cabinet can go to its new— or old— home without you."

She wanted to stay, too. "Send it. I'll think about the rest."

"That should be time enough to answer some important questions— and to change your mind about ever leaving me."

She didn't know how she stayed on her feet. Her lungs couldn't draw air, and her heart pounded against her ribs hard enough to break them. Holt really did want her. He would never make a declaration like that if he was unsure. She knew he was watching her, waiting for a reaction, a few words to reassure him, or tell him she didn't want a future with him. But try as she might, she couldn't get any words past the lump in her throat. She swallowed, trying to clear it.

"I'll let you think about it," Holt finally said, but the uncertainty in his eyes wounded her.

"I...I dinna need to," she finally voiced. "I dinna want to leave ye. Ye surprised me."

His shoulders dropped and his relief made her want to sag into his arms, but she stood her ground, waiting for him to make the first move.

"I'm falling in love with ye, Caitlin. I know it's sudden, but in my life, I've never felt anything like what I feel for you. I don't even care if you don't feel the same—yet. But I hope you will. I know you care."

"I do, Holt. More than ye ken."

He reached for her then. "I can hear it in your voice.

Your accent gets strong when you get emotional. That's enough for me. For now."

~

The next day, after the storm broke, Holt took Caitlin to the village. Memories came flooding back the moment he stepped into the village library he'd driven by a few days ago and opted not to enter. The smells were the same. Books. Musty, dusty books by the thousands. The metal carts his mother used to push around while she re-shelved books were still there. Only she was missing. He took a breath, willing away the melancholy that washed through him. She was gone. This wasn't their place any longer. It was just a library, valuable in its own right, but no longer hers. Or his.

At the desk, Caitlin asked the librarian about yearbooks.

Something seemed wrong until he realized the scent of old Mrs. Dunmore's flowery perfume was missing. As a child, every time he approached this desk, the heavy sweetness surrounding the librarian made him sneeze. And yet today, he missed it.

The only smell he detected now, besides books, was the warm one that always said *Caitlin* to him. He focused on her, his lifeline in the sea of memories swamping him.

The current librarian appeared to be only a few years older than he was. He was dimly aware of the woman pointing them to a set of stacks on the far side of the room.

"We can find it," Caitlin assured the woman. "Thanks."

Holt followed her past the scarred wooden study tables and a new-looking row of digital workstations and monitors.

"All the latest gear," Caitlin commented as they passed.

"The library certainly had nothing like those when I was a kid," Holt said in agreement.

"Times change," Caitlin responded and led him toward the stacks. "Did you spend a lot of time here?"

Did he? Only the best time, as it turned out. "Yes. My mother worked here part-time so I could read all the books I wanted."

"Is that how she supported you?"

"She worked as a bookkeeper for an accounting firm a few miles from here. I drove over this way a few days ago, the day I got back from the city, but so much has changed, I couldn't bring myself to come in here." Something seemed to lighten within him with that admission, and the next. "I only found one friend from high school at the pizza place his family owns, but none of her friends or coworkers. No one to shed any light."

"I'm sorry. I know this is hard." She paused before one of a long row of wooden shelves bowed by the weight of the tomes they carried. Yearbooks. "Maybe these books will help. Look familiar?"

Not really. Here was something else that brought home how little he knew about his mother's past. He ran a finger across the spines, studying the dates, heart sinking. "I don't see the volume for the year she graduated."

"What about the year before?"

Holt traced a finger across the volumes until he found

the right one. He pulled it from the shelf and flipped pages. "Senior class…ah, Junior class…"

"Let me see, too!"

In another circumstance, Caitlin's demand might have amused him, but he was suddenly awash with tension. What would they find? It was just a book, but it might hold a clue to his past. His father. His mother's friends. He stepped to a mostly empty shelf and laid the book open on it. Caitlin crowded close as he turned pages. Then he was there. His mother's picture all but leapt from the page. Jennifer Cooper, in a black portrait-neckline top, long blonde hair covering her shoulders. And right before her on the same row, James Coates, looking like he'd rather be anywhere else, in a shirt collar a size too small, tie and suit jacket. And no other Coopers at all.

Caitlin pointed. "They did know each other. He told me," she reminded him, "they were in the same class."

"Apparently." Holt's eyes brimmed with moisture, and he looked away, determined to keep Caitlin from noticing how seeing his mother and the boy who would honorably serve his country, then become a veterinarian— after possibly becoming his father— affected him. "But it proves nothing."

"Keep going. If they include class activities or clubs, there might be pictures of them together with other friends."

He paged past the younger classes to the clubs and athletic team photos but found nothing, then closed the book with a dull thud and took it back to the shelf where it belonged. He didn't know what he'd expected to find, so he couldn't put a finger on why he felt so disappointed, but he did. "We need to talk to Doc Coates."

"Now?"

Caitlin's voice intruded on his glum mood, and he welcomed the distraction. "Why not?"

She glanced at her phone. "This time of day, he'll likely be at the practice. If not, they'll know where to find him." Caitlin's eyes sparkled.

With excitement or determination? Or both? Either way, Holt knew neither of them would be satisfied until they solved the riddle of the vet and his mother. "Let's go."

"He's on his lunch break," the receptionist, Rachel, told them when they arrived. "But I'll let him know you're here."

Moments later, she led them back to Doc Coates's office, along with the swarm of bees buzzing around in Holt's gut. Now that they were in the veterinary practice, with its smells of dogs, cats, and disinfectants, Holt's belly was less sure this course of action was a wise one. Too late.

The man Caitlin presumed to be his father stood as they entered. A half-eaten sandwich and cup of coffee sat on one side of his desk. Paperwork cluttered the center. He smiled at Caitlin, then raised an eyebrow at Holt. "Caitlin! What brings you in today?"

"Sorry to interrupt, Doc. You remember Holt Ridley? We…"

Caitlin trailed off and glanced around at Holt. Taking

pity on her, he picked up the conversational thread. "We just came from the library, where we took a look at my mother's junior-year yearbook. You and she were classmates."

"Oh? Who was she?"

"Jennifer Cooper. Your picture is right next to hers in the book."

The doc's gaze dropped to the desk, and his cheeks colored, then he met Holt's gaze. "I knew her well. We were friends…"

"And more?" Caitlin asked.

Her directness surprised Holt, and apparently the doc as well. He waited a beat before answering.

"Yes, I suppose you could say that. Before I left for the Army, we were pretty tight. She was popular— not that way. She cared about people in general, but she only had a few really close friends. They're all gone now. I've checked."

Gone now. The phrase resonated with something Mrs. Smith had said. Her son had been killed, and he'd lived right there in the same house as Holt's mother. What if they were wrong about Doc Coates?

"Did you know she got pregnant?" Caitlin again, bless her, determined as ever to fight his battles for him. Why had he not seen that sooner? Everything she'd done since he met her, she'd done for him.

The doc's eyes widened, and he shook his head.

Today, it appeared, was a day for Holt's eyes to open, or for his brain to start exploring alternatives. "She had a son," Holt told him, his blood suddenly running with chips of ice in his veins. So much depended on how this went. "Me. My birthday is a little less than nine months after her graduation."

Doc frowned and lowered himself to his chair, nodding for them to take the visitors' chairs on the other side of his desk. "Are you saying what I think you're saying?" He shook his head. "Stupid question. Of course you are." He studied Holt for a moment. "You look like her, you know."

"I've been told that."

"A DNA test will prove the connection…or not. I can arrange it."

"Good," Caitlin interrupted. "And we'll do another at a separate lab, just so there's no question."

"I think I've been insulted."

Holt glanced at Caitlin. He'd said he wanted only one, but here and now, he saw the sense of what she proposed. "Not really," Holt interjected. "There are other factors to consider. For one, I'm wealthy. Very. I have to be sure of the people around me. I'm sorry, but it's a fact of my life."

Doc nodded but didn't say anything. He looked to Holt like someone trying desperately to make sense of the sudden change in his world and not having much luck.

"You never knew?" Holt asked though the answer was obvious from Doc's demeanor.

"I spent decades away, out of touch with anyone here. But, funny thing, Jenny was what brought me back. Memories of my time in school with her. Being here with her was the happiest I've been in my life. Until my father made it impossible." He shrugged. "Or so I thought. Granted, I expected to find her still in the area, married and with a houseful of kids, so I was shocked and saddened to find her gone. Her aunt told me she'd died."

"Not then, but six years ago."

Doc's frown turned icy. "That old…she lied. And I believed her." He leaned his elbows on the desk and clasped his hands together in front of his mouth. "Why would I doubt what Jenny's family told me?" He clenched and unclenched his fists. "All that time—." He sat back and paused again; regret written clearly in the set of his mouth. "That's all I knew. I should have talked to others in our class. Friends of ours. Of hers. Maybe they would have told me she'd had a son. Possibly my son." He met Holt's gaze again. "If it's true you're mine, we have a lot of catching up to do."

"I'm sorry to spring this on you so suddenly. This has to be a shock for you," Caitlin said.

Doc's lips pressed together, then he blew out a breath. "If it is true, I'm damn sorry to have missed so much of your life, Holt. Not to have been there for you. For Jenny, when she needed me. She took it hard when her parents were killed in that car crash. She wasn't happy living with her aunt."

"After she started showing, her aunt kicked her out," Holt said as the old resentment flared anew in his gut. "She raised me alone, a single mother, denied and disinherited by the only family she had left. She told me my father died. I guess she never knew where you went, why you disappeared so suddenly. You were her friend, and maybe more. But you disappeared."

Doc rubbed his hands over his face. "My God." After

another moment, he took a breath and spoke. "It's a long story, but the condensed version is I left after a fight with my father, signed up at the local recruiting center, and shipped out the next day." His fist clenched. "I could have found a way to tell her I was leaving and why. I should have. Then she would have had a chance to tell me— but I was so angry with my father, my focus was totally on packing my stuff and getting the hell out of town. I was still a kid. I wasn't thinking about anyone but myself." He shook his head. "If I'd had any inkling that my actions would affect two other people, ruin two other lives— I have no excuse. I only wish I could go back and make it right."

Holt had a touch of the temper Doc Coates described, too. Caitlin shared a look with him that said *are you hearing this?* He gave her a nod. From her son, Mrs. Smith had known about fights Holt had with his father. Here was another indication that the work Caitlin had done had gotten him on the right track.

He was impressed with the vet's willingness to consider their claim, and how his story aligned with what little they knew about Holt's mother's history, but he wasn't yet ready to let the man off the hook. Holt could admit that in balance, his life hadn't been ruined. He'd made the most of the hand he'd been dealt. But his mother's? Hers had been destroyed, first by her parents' deaths, then by her aunt who tossed her out with the trash when she got pregnant with him. He spoke before he could let anger overtake him. "Can you take the DNA samples here?"

Doc stood and motioned toward the door. "I've got kits

in the lab. It'll take five minutes, and then, I hate to do this given what we've been talking about, but I've got to get back to work. I've got a surgery scheduled in a few minutes. The usual— a dog hit by a car. I was grabbing lunch while the techs prepped him."

"Let's do the kits and get out of your way," Caitlin prompted.

"We can talk more when the results come back," Holt agreed, hoping after the news they'd just given him, the vet's hands would be steady enough to do the surgery the dog needed.

True to the doc's word, in five minutes, they were headed out the door, a set of samples in hand to deliver to a different lab than the vet used. His father. Maybe. Despite everything, Holt found himself hoping it was true.

CHAPTER 12

"You look like you found coal in your stocking."

Caitlin jumped in surprise at the sound of Holt's voice as he entered the office the next morning, coffee cup in hand. She inhaled the enticing aroma. "Is that for me? I beat Mrs. Smith to the kitchen this morning. The tea I brewed is hours cold." She'd forgotten it. She'd been hard at work, putting more finishing touches on the catalog that would result in the sale of many of the treasures in the estate.

"Take this one. I can get another." Holt set the cup on her worktable, his generosity an indication of the change in him since she'd first met him. Perhaps yesterday's revelations, and the concrete step of doing the DNA tests, had a lot to do with it, but he'd been warming up to her and to this place since their discoveries in the attic.

He moved around the cluttered surface to look over her shoulder.

She wasn't sure how she felt about the catalog anymore.

True, she'd come here to do a job, and though she'd disagreed with Holt about the need for it, she'd done it well. But something in her couldn't take pride in it. She hated to see the collection scattered to the four winds, the estate sold, and all of Holt's family history, good and bad, out of his hands. "Thanks for the coffee." After a sip that warmed her and chased away some of her dismay in pure, caffeinated pleasure, she added, "I don't have a stocking," in response to the first thing he'd said when he came in the door. "None of us do."

He shifted and rested one hip on the desk. Then he quirked an eyebrow at her. "We need to fix that."

"What? Celebrate Christmas? In this house? Who are you and what have you done with Holt Ridley?"

"It's time, don't you think? Christmas is two days away, and this old place needs some cheering up." He glanced upward, as if staring through the ceiling. "We found several boxes of decorations in the attic. Let's use them."

Caitlin pushed up from her chair. Holt stood, too, and she threw herself into his arms. "That's a brilliant idea. Let's do."

"In a moment," Holt said and dipped his head.

His lips met hers, tasting of coffee and him. Caitlin tightened her hold on his shoulders, her knees too weak to support her weight as his lips moved over hers, teasing, coaxing, surprising her. The man could kiss! Better than she'd imagined that day on the beach. If this Holt was what she'd been missing, she regretted not acting on her impulse then. His arms wrapped her body like steel bands and held her against his solid strength. She could stay here forever, feeling the tip of his tongue grazing her mouth, his lips on her throat, his teeth nipping her earlobe before his mouth took hers, again.

She tunneled her fingers in his hair and kissed him back, heat sizzling through her veins and melting her core. When his tongue breached the barrier of her lips, she moaned and pulled him closer, sliding her hands down his back to his firm arse.

Holt growled and did the same, pressing her close and making his arousal unmistakable. By the time he broke the kiss, they were both panting and flushed, eyes dark with desire.

Caitlin rested her head on his shoulder for a moment, then pulled away, reminding herself she was leaving for Scotland in a few days and might never see this man again. A few hot kisses were one thing, but getting more involved than that? Regret made her tone bleak. "We shouldn't."

Holt brushed her hair back and nodded. "Not yet." He gusted out a breath. "But soon. In the meantime, we have decorating to do." He flashed her one of his rare grins.

Soon? She could have floated as she led Holt up the attic stairs, never touching a tread. *Soon* carried a lot of meanings, a lot of expectations, and possibly a lot of happiness. Though she knew better than to act on it, she could enjoy the daydream.

In the meantime, his eagerness to find the boxes of garlands, colored balls, wreaths, stockings, and all the other things his great-aunt had used to decorate the estate surprised and pleased her. She stopped halfway up the steps and twisted around. "Ach, nay. We don't have a tree."

"We can get one," Holt assured her. "Or dispense with that this year and just use whatever strikes your fancy."

This year, the man said. Did that mean next year— with her— was also on his mind? "So, you," she teased, "draped across the mantle?"

"I can think of somewhere more comfortable than a mantle I'd rather be— but anywhere will do as long as you're there with me."

Caitlin laughed, hoping he meant what he said but afraid to take him too seriously. She wagged a finger at him, then bounded up the rest of the stairs. "First, we have to find those stockings!"

An hour later, boxes littered the front hallway, and both she and Holt were covered in dust. They'd found the stockings and hung them on the front room fireplace mantel. Scattered ribbons and bows and decorative balls were on the floor where Caitlin had dropped them while digging through the boxes. "Where is the garland these go on? And wreaths for the front door?"

"What are you two doing?" Mrs. Smith's stunned voice echoed as she marched into the foyer from the long hallway leading from the kitchen, fists on hips.

Caitlin and Holt exchanged sheepish glances. "We wanted to find stockings to hang on the hearth," she explained. "But there are no wreaths or swag in these boxes to decorate anything else."

"That's because every year, Farrell and I get them from the local farmers— fresh evergreens, mind you— and use all of those…things you've scattered about to make them festive. Given the circumstances and Mr. Ridley's disinterest, we didn't acquire any this year."

"Mr. Ridley's disinterest has taken a hike," Holt replied with a grin. He brushed back his hair and left a smear of gray dust on his forehead.

"Are fresh evergreens still available?" Caitlin asked.

"Here and there," Mrs. Smith answered, crossing her arms. "Though we might need to take a ride up to the north fork. There are more farm stands up there."

"We'll go," Caitlin volunteered.

"No, dear. You won't know where to go. Farrell and I are old hands at this. We'll go and be back before you could even find the north fork."

Holt grinned at Caitlin. "I think we've been insulted. Or was that a challenge?"

Mrs. Smith shook her head. "If you want to do something to create some holiday cheer," she said and gestured at the mess they'd made of the front foyer, "it'll be easier to find what we want to decorate with if you'll pick up all that and box like things with like." She turned to go, then turned back. "Oh, and there are sandwiches on the kitchen table when you get hungry." She left them to do as she asked.

Holt watched her go, an odd half-smile on his face.

Caitlin couldn't resist the urge to find out what caused it. "Penny for your thoughts?"

"I thought I was the boss here."

"Nay, laddie, nay. Not when Mrs. Smith is around."

Holt laughed, and they bent to clear away the mess they'd made, Caitlin's mind on Mrs. Smith. What if she was his grandmother? She didn't think he would mind. Would Mrs. Smith? If the DNA results with Doc Coates were disappointing, she'd ask her.

~

After cleaning up the mess they'd made and eating the lunch Mrs. Smith had left them, Caitlin went back to work on her catalog. Holt left for an appointment in town, one he was looking forward to for a change. He had in mind a contingency— one he hadn't discussed with Caitlin. It was something that, if it came to pass, he thought she'd approve. But he needed to discuss it with Mr. Thornton. That, and the holiday bonuses for Mrs. Smith and Farrell. He planned to make their Christmas very, very merry.

After the lawyer confirmed that what Holt wanted to do would take some paperwork, but it could be done, Holt decided he'd put off long enough the most difficult visit of all. If he hurried, he could accomplish it and return to the estate before dark.

Still, he couldn't make himself go directly there. Instead of taking the main route toward the village, he took side roads, cruising through neighborhoods and eventually, through Sag Harbor on the road to the bridge to Shelter Island and beyond it, the north fork. Farrell and Mrs. Smith had gone up there after holiday greenery. The wine the estate served for dinner, which had been unfailingly good, also came from there. But going in search of the winery would take hours. A distraction, nothing more.

Instead of continuing, he turned off onto the Long Beach Road and followed it until he saw sand and water.

He pulled off in a parking lot and lowered the car's windows to breathe in the scent of water, trees, and sunshine. For a few minutes, he watched children in rolled-up pants chase each other as ducks glided out of their reach in the cold shallows, and parents sitting on beach towels keeping their gazes on every move their offspring made. It struck him that those kids were enjoying life more fully and easily than he had at that age. In this place. But how much of what he thought he remembered was real, and how much was colored by his family history?

He started the car and followed the road until he could turn east, then south. Before he knew it, he recognized the turnoff to the cemetery. He pulled up to the entrance and stopped, still reluctant. But it was time. Past time. He pulled forward. Inside the gates, much had changed over the years, but he found his mother's marker easily, nonetheless. He'd insisted she be laid to rest on a knoll under a tree, giving her the view of forest, sky, and, if he squinted, a sliver of ocean. The kind of view she'd missed after her aunt threw her out like common trash. He'd made enough money to give her the view in a high-end condo during her last year of life— though the thing she'd wanted most, him nearby, had been impossible by then. His company took all his time and energy. If he'd known he'd lose her so soon, would he have done anything differently? Come east more often? Flown her out to see him? He hoped so.

"Hello, Mama. I'm here." He knelt and laid a hand on the headstone. *Jennifer Cooper Ridley*, it read. *Beloved Mother* as she'd requested. Her final shot at her aunt— as if that woman would have ever visited this grave and seen the inscription. But perhaps someone told the old witch about the epitaph. That would have been enough.

"You won't believe *why* I'm here." He paused and looked around him, feeling foolish, yet needing to say what he now realized he'd come here to say. To ask. "I'm sure you haven't seen your Aunt Amelia where you are, so she hasn't had a chance to torment you." He paused to clear his suddenly tight throat. "But you need to know, she left me everything she denied you. You know I don't want it. I'm going to get rid of all of it as fast as I can, one way or another. But I need to know, does *everything* include the curse you told me about? I never really believed in it, but whether it's real or not is starting to matter to me. A lot."

She didn't answer. Of course not. Holt was crazy to be talking to her headstone, much less to be talking to her headstone about a nearly three-hundred-year-old curse. Even crazier to expect an answer.

But if something as crazy as a family curse could be real, perhaps so could this sudden sense of disquiet piercing his grief. Was that her answer?

After another moment of silence, he stood and turned to squint at the horizon, looking for that sliver of sea. He missed it, lost in a low bank of sea fog that had yet to make it onto shore. *He missed her.* She'd done the best she could, raising a gifted son alone. He hadn't been able to repay a fraction of what he owed her. He never would. Guilt filled him. There was so much more he could have done, if only he'd known how limited their time together would be. So much more he should have done. But he could get on with his life and make it better than hers had been. She would want that. Not the money necessarily, but the family, friends, and loved ones. Children chasing ducks in the cold water at the shore.

If Caitlin was right, he could have all of that. When he'd threatened to send her home, she'd said she had only wanted to help, to bring him some happiness. She'd thought she'd ruined everything. She was wrong. She'd helped. She'd made him feel…something. Happiness? He wasn't sure, but he was sure she'd given him hope. "There's a woman, Mama. Her name is Caitlin Paterson, and I know you'd love her. I want to take care of her. I'm going to do everything in my power to have a long, happy life with her. I hope you'll give us your blessing."

～

"Thank you, dear, for sorting the holiday ornaments," Mrs. Smith said, surveying the neat array of boxes lining the entry foyer's walls.

Caitlin stepped away from the office door and followed the older woman down the hall. She was surprised at how long it had taken Mrs. Smith and Farrell to return from their errand to the north fork. She'd heard their voices in the kitchen and left her worktable to go see what they'd brought. But Mrs. Smith's hands were empty, and Caitlin didn't smell any fresh pine or greenery. "Were the stands you went to visit closed?"

"Oh, no. Farrell is bringing in what we found, with Mr. Ridley's help."

"Holt is back? He's been gone nearly as long as you were."

"Well, everyone is here now, so we can begin to decorate, but perhaps," she said, glancing at her watch, "after I make us a light supper. We'll enjoy it more on a full stomach, don't you think?"

"That's a great idea," Holt said, coming down the hall from the kitchen, a large wreath in each hand. "I'm hungry. Judging by what I see Farrell unloading outside, I suspect you and he are, too. Caitlin?"

"I can sign up for that. In the meantime, Holt and I will finish bringing in everything else."

"Farrell can get it," Mrs. Smith objected.

"Not if he wants supper any time soon," Holt said. "It's more than a one-person job. We'll help."

Mrs. Smith gave him a grateful smile and took a step toward the kitchen. "Supper will be ready in thirty minutes."

Holt turned his attention to Caitlin, making her face warm at the way his gaze raked her body.

"You'd better put on something else," he told her, shattering the illusion of his interest, "unless you want those clothes covered in sap and pine needles."

She nodded. "I'll go change and meet you outside."

By the time Caitlin joined the men at the back door, they'd stacked more pine wreathes and roping nearby and were discussing the best way to bring the large fir tree tied atop the estate's oversized truck into the house.

"I've got stands in the workroom at the end of the garages," Farrell was saying, "but we need to trim the base and get it in water right after."

"You know where they are. Why don't you get the tools you need," Holt told him. "Caitlin and I will pull the tree trunk far enough out of the tailgate for you to do the trimming."

Farrell nodded and headed across the car park between the house and the set of garages.

Holt turned to her and grinned. "Ready for some tug-o-war?"

"Tugging on that?" She walked around the truck's bed, sizing up the future Yule tree. With its limbs bound up for transport, it looked massive as well as tall, tied up over the truck's cab. "How did you get it up there in the first place?"

"With help," Holt admitted. "Mrs. Smith wanted a tree tall enough for the entryway, and a shorter one for the front room."

"There are two trees in there?"

Holt grimaced and nodded. "The smaller one is underneath." He studied their handiwork for a moment, then swore. "We can't move anything until those lines are cut. It was tied down tight for the drive back."

"Let's take the truck around to the front entrance," Farrell said, approaching them, a toolbox in one strong hand, a smaller tree stand under one arm and the larger one in his other hand.

"While you lads work on that, I'll start moving the greenery indoors," Caitlin offered.

Farrell shook his head. "It'll be better off out here. The

cold will keep it fresher, and it'll be damp tonight as well. In the house, it would dry out before Mrs. Smith could decide how to use it."

As soon as the taller tree's trunk was trimmed and they'd placed it in its stand in the foyer, Mrs. Smith called them for dinner. "Ah, that looks grand," she exclaimed, a twinkle in her eye. "Now, eat first, then you can bring in the smaller one."

After the meal and the smaller tree was set up, she set Caitlin and Holt to work decorating the trees while she worked on the wreaths Holt brought in earlier— and she directed them.

Caitlin had to admit she was having fun. Holt looked relaxed and happy, too. Especially when she had to climb the ladder to reach the upper part of the tree. He helped her up and steadied it, then helped her back down again, touching her more than he ever had at one time. She quite liked it. From the way his gaze darkened, he did, too. Out of sight of Mrs. Smith, behind the tree, he even snuck a few quick kisses.

Caitlin decided she rather much liked an American Christmas.

By the time the trees were done, Caitlin was elated— and exhausted. Holt looked drawn, and both Mrs. Smith and Farrell had left them alone thirty minutes earlier to go to their own beds. Caitlin settled on the foyer steps and patted the space beside her for Holt.

"Isn't it beautiful?" The tree glowed with multicolored lights and glints of shiny glass ornaments among the boughs. Beyond it, in the front room, the smaller tree took pride of place in front of the window. Both trees would be visible to anyone approaching the house. A signal that things were improving in the estate, or so Caitlin hoped.

Holt nodded, his gaze on the trees, then he turned to her and took her hand. "Thank you for this."

"Me? You were the one who agreed we should get the boxes of decorations down from the attic."

"I did, didn't I?" He looked satisfied with himself.

Caitlin stifled a laugh.

"And do you know what the best part of that decision is?" At her quizzical look, he raised their joined hands. "Spending time with you, doing something fun. Not working, not digging through history. Just…being. A few weeks ago, I wouldn't have thought I was capable of that. Of enjoying that. Thank you."

"You're welcome." She met his serious gaze with one of her own. "It was always in you. You just needed time away from everything in your past, your work, that lawsuit. Even though your past here wasn't happy—"

"It wasn't always unhappy. And you have added a fresh layer of good memories."

"Then my work here is done," Caitlin joked and immediately regretted it. Done meant free to return to Scotland. To leave Holt. The thought hollowed her insides.

Holt used his free hand to cup her cheek. "I'm a work in progress, don't you think? I need you. I don't want you to go." He leaned in slowly, his gaze never leaving her eyes, until his breath warmed her face, and his lips caressed hers.

Caitlin let her eyes drift closed and simply enjoyed Holt's kiss. Hiding quick pecks from Mrs. Smith had been fun, but this was something else entirely. She could feel the intensity of Holt's focus on her in the way his lips moved over hers, then trailed across her cheek. He needed her. What a change from the arrogant, distant man she'd first met to the one now gently nibbling her earlobe. Caitlin let her head fall back on a sigh, giving him access to her skin, and to her racing pulse. He pulled her against his chest as he kissed his way down her throat. She needed him, too. More than he kenned.

~

Caitlin welcomed Christmas Eve's calm and cold. Last week's storms had mirrored the conflict between her and Holt. But they'd made peace in time for and in the spirit of the holiday.

Holt drove them into the village in silence. Caitlin knew he had to be nervous, but so was she. They'd heard from the lab Holt had chosen and planned to meet Doc Coates at the village square Christmas celebration to open and share the report Holt received. The vet had mentioned that he would be there, along with most of the rest of the village.

On the outskirts, Holt broke his silence and told her, "I had a thought."

"I hope you didn't strain anything."

He cut her a side-eyed glance. "Again, not funny. Are there any funny people in Scotland? I'd like to meet one."

"Sorry, you're out of luck. You're stuck with me. So, what thought?"

"About what to do if this report doesn't confirm a match."

Caitlin's chest tightened with sympathy for what he must be going through. "I might have had the same thought," she told him. "You first."

Holt slowed, then stopped to let some people cross the street. "Mrs. Smith's son is also dead. He lived in the same house. He and my mother were friends. Sometimes proximity and teenage hormones…"

"We're in sync. But let's see what the report you received says. If we're wrong, we can approach Mrs. Smith about testing her."

Holt accelerated smoothly once the street cleared. "She might like having me as a grandson."

"Of course she would. You're adorable. And that would give her an excuse to shop for toys."

"*So* not funny." But he grinned at her.

Relieved that her attempt at humor had eased his worries, she settled back to enjoy the town lights and the glimpses of Christmas trees in cottage front windows.

They parked a few blocks away from the square and walked back, drawn by even more lights, colorful and white, the holiday music, and the sound of laughter. Scents both savory and sweet filled their nostrils as soon as they reached it.

"It's lovely," Caitlin remarked as they circled the huge central fir tree, fully decked out in lights, garlands, and ornaments— many handmade by local school children. "Though not as special as the trees we decorated at the house," she told him, the memory of that evening still fresh and happy in her mind. The smile Holt gave her told her he felt the same way.

Singing drew them to one side of the square, where carolers in Elizabethan garb entertained the crowd. They listened for a while, then wandered on, admiring the holiday displays set up by local businesses in their front windows. Holt bought them hot chocolate to keep them warm. It didn't compare to Mrs. Smith's, but it took the edge off the chill in Caitlin's fingers.

Finally, they found an empty bench in a quiet corner of the square and sat down. They hadn't seen Doc Coates yet, but Caitlin was confident he would show up soon.

"Caitlin," Holt said, startling her out of her thoughts. "I owe you an apology."

"For what?" She was genuinely puzzled. He hadn't done anything worthy of begging her forgiveness— at least not today.

"For— everything. For not believing you. Not trusting you. I should have seen that everything you've said and done since I met you was meant to help me."

"It took you long enough," Caitlin muttered, injecting as much irony in her tone as she could manage and hoping he'd take it as a jest. She understood his pensive mood and wanted to cheer him. It was Christmas, after all.

Instead, he ignored her response. "You've been nothing but truthful with me, and you've stood your ground when I...when I gave you a bunch of crap you didn't deserve. No matter what happens with the paternity test, I want you to know I appreciate everything you've done. I think you're an amazing woman."

She set aside her drink. It had gone cold. But the sudden chill in her chest was colder. What was Holt leading up to? It almost sounded like he was getting ready to say goodbye. The bulk of her work was done, and the rest she could finish at home. He knew that. Was he circling around to sending her away, as he had planned to before the storms gave them time to remember they liked each other? A lot? "Aye. I know that," she replied, still going for humor, though it now felt out of place after his heartfelt words.

"Humble, too," he added on a sudden grin.

Caitlin smirked back, relieved. She hadn't misjudged what he needed from her, and his grin reassured her that she hadn't jumped to the wrong conclusion. "What are you trying to tell me, Holt?"

He put his cup on the ground and faced her. "That we're running out of time, and I'm in love with you." He paused and studied her.

Caitlin held her breath, torn between the joy filling her and the impossibility of that love leading to a future with this man.

"I want you to know that," Holt continued before she could gather her wits to form a reply. "I never expected…I guess you never know when it's going to happen. When you find love. I know I have." He brushed a bit of wind-blown hair off of her cheek. "I hope you feel the same way."

Caitlin's heart stopped, then beat a frantic pace in her chest, sending her blood pulsing to her extremities. Heat and cold washed through her, one after the other, over and over. She did feel the same, but she'd never expected to hear those words from the very guarded Holt Ridley. And not at a time like this, when he was about to discover if his life would include a father he'd never known.

"Caitlin? Say something." He reached for her, but when she didn't answer immediately, he drew back.

"I do," she choked out around the lump in her throat. "Feel the same way, I mean." Caitlin coughed and waved a hand in front of her face when Holt reached for her. "I'm in love with ye, too. I just didn't expect—"

"That I could let you inside my walls? I'm surprised about that, too."

"And that ye could ever say the words." She took a steadying breath, swallowed, and touched his arm. "You're right. You don't get to choose when you find love. But you do get to choose what to do about it. So, what shall we do? I live in Scotland, and you in California. Or here. I—"

"Not here," he replied just as a fireworks display lit the night sky in the direction of the harbor. "But we can work something out. As long as we choose each other. Six months in each?"

Caitlin's gaze was drawn to the bright display. It was impossible to ignore the booms as each burst showered colored lights down onto the village. "That would be horribly expen—"

"I can handle it."

"Ach, aye. I guess I don't know how to imagine living with that kind of wealth."

"But you'll enjoy learning."

Caitlin twisted on the bench to face him. "I don't care about that. I care about you."

"I know, and I'm grateful. I want—"

A hoarse shout rose above the background noise of Christmas music and the happy rumble of many voices in the square reacting to the display above them. Then a scream sounded and shocked silence followed for a moment before voices resumed, tense and urgent.

"What's happening?" Caitlin asked, jumping to her feet and trying to see where the commotion was coming from. The colorful lights on the central tree took on a surreal haze as smoke from the fireworks drifted past.

Holt stood beside her as more shouts filled the night, then he grabbed her hand and tugged her in that direction. They passed frantic mothers rushing children out of the square. Others, mostly men and teenagers paralleled their path toward the disturbance. Something had happened to destroy the joyful celebration, and the lights and faltering music suddenly seemed out of place. Caitlin dreaded what they might see. "Did the fireworks set something ablaze?" Had someone been hurt? Or killed?

In moments, they spotted a tattered-looking man waving a butcher knife and sobbing in front of the huge, central Christmas tree. Medals and military insignia covered the faded fabric of his ragged jacket.

"What the hell?" Holt had barely uttered the words when a town constable appeared, waving people back from the vicinity of the tree. He must have ordered the fireworks paused because they sputtered to a stop and the square got quiet except for the sound of voices raised in fear. Mutterings reached her, something about a homeless vet, but that was all she understood. How sad.

The constable approached the man, speaking to him in a voice too low to understand from where she and Holt stood. But when the man waved his knife in an arc in front of him, then brought it up to his own throat, the constable stopped several meters away.

"No!" Caitlin breathed. "He can't do that. My God, there are children everywhere."

What had driven this man to such a desperate act? And why here? And now? If he had fought for his country, surely he would want to protect the children who flocked to an event such as this. Had the fireworks triggered something within him that he couldn't control?

She spotted Doc Coates approach on the constable's other side and give them a nod of recognition. She clutched Holt's arm, but in this situation, all thoughts of their purpose in coming to meet him to reveal the results of the paternity tests fled.

Doc Coates spoke urgently to the constable for several moments, low enough that she couldn't hear what he was saying. But he must have convinced the constable of something. The man nodded and Doc Coates turned and made a quick gesture behind him.

A medium-sized mixed-breed dog approached the distraught man, long floppy ears bouncing as it trotted forward. The dog stopped a pace away in front of him and sat, looked up with sad eyes and whined.

Caitlin held her breath. What would the man do? Was the dog in danger? Would Doc Coates have sent it forward if he thought it could be harmed? She felt Holt shift his stance beside her, tension apparent in the stiffness of the arm brushing hers, but she couldn't look away from the tableau in front of the tree to check on Holt.

Surprised or distracted by the dog's approach and friendly demeanor, the distraught man lowered the knife from his throat. He made no other threatening move. He simply held the blade against his chest, his gaze on the dog.

Caitlin feared the constable would rush the man while the dog distracted him, but he didn't. The dog stood and stepped forward, never taking its gaze from the man. When the man didn't move, the dog licked the empty hand by his side and pushed against his leg, nuzzling him, then licked his hand again. Time seemed to freeze as the dog gazed up into the man's tortured face.

The man tossed the knife aside and fell to his knees. He wrapped his arms around the dog, smothering sobs in its soft fur.

Caitlin let out the breath she hadn't realized she was holding.

The dog squirmed in delight, yipped, and licked tears from the man's face as fast as it could. It tried so hard to snuggle with the man that it pushed him onto his side, then relaxed and rested, wrapped in his arms.

The constable approached then, but he only picked up the knife. He gave the man a few minutes with the dog, then spoke softly to him. The man sat up, took the dog's head in his hands and rested his forehead on the dog's, then let the constable help him to his feet and take charge of him.

Doc Coates called the dog back to his side where Holt and Caitlin joined him.

"You did that," Caitlin said, marveling. "How did you know the dog would calm him down?"

Doc Coates' gaze was on the constable and his charge. "It's what I do. In addition to the rescue work you know about, I'm training some of the dogs for just this sort of crisis. To help vets, homeless or not, who are suffering with PTSD."

"How did you know?" Holt repeated Caitlin's earlier question.

Doc Coates clearly understood his intent. "The fireworks."

"I've never seen anything like that," Holt said. "You saved that man's life. He looked ready to cut his own throat."

Doc Coates reached down and rubbed the dog's head. "Not me. The constable gave him the space he needed for Chauncey to save him. We just happened to be in the right place at the right time."

CHAPTER 13

Holt couldn't believe what he'd just seen—what the man who might be his father had accomplished. "All that took was a quick gesture to a friendly dog," he said.

"And weeks of training beforehand," Doc Coates answered with a smile, turning to meet Holt's gaze. "To protect the man, of course, but also the dog if the man failed to respond and threatened him."

Chauncey looked up in adoration, tongue lolling, and panting with excitement. "You did a good job, boy," the Doc said, crouching down to hug the dog. "You saved a life tonight." He spent a few moments there, continuing to pet the dog, then stood.

Other people approached then, voicing their amazement and congratulations. Holt's heart swelled with pride. Whether this man was his father or not, he was glad to know him.

Once the crowd around them and Chauncey thinned

and drifted back to the Christmas-themed events, Caitlin caught Holt's gaze, her expression uncertain.

Was this still the right time to share the report he'd received and answer the question of his parentage? He wanted to know, but after what they'd just witnessed, would a negative result be too much of a disappointment? Also for the man who might be his father? Given what he had just achieved and Coates' calm response to the event and the accolades from the village that followed it, Holt was certain Doc Coates would be able to handle anything. Holt nodded.

Caitlin took and breath and spoke up. "Did you get a lab report yet?"

Doc Coates turned his gaze back to Holt and held it for a moment. "I did. You did, as well?"

Holt nodded, the euphoria of the recent excitement fading. "Haven't opened it yet."

"Nor have I." Doc pulled an envelope out of an inside pocket and proffered it.

Holt traded it for the one that had come to him. "This seems as good a time and place as any…" Christmas lights, Caitlin by his side, and a life just saved all seemed good omens. He feared the hope that was blooming in his chest. No, he didn't fear the hope. He feared losing it if the reports didn't— no, he wouldn't think that way.

When Doc Coates nodded, Holt ripped open the envelope and pulled out a single folded sheet of paper.

Doc did the same, eyed him, and opened the form.

With a glance aside at Caitlin, Holt unfolded his. He didn't look at the report right away. Caitlin's expression captured his attention. Her eyes were shining, and she smiled encouragement at him. He nodded and looked down but couldn't focus on the writing. He blinked, trying to clear his vision. It was hopeless. He was too wound up. Everything appeared watery. Instead of fighting it, he handed her the paper. "Read it, please. I can't."

Doc Coates also passed the report he held to her. "Please."

Caitlin's eyes closed for a moment, as if weighing the responsibility of delivering the results she knew meant so much to both men. Then she looked down at the papers in her hands.

Holt watched as Caitlin studied first one form, then the other, her eyes growing wider as she read. Then she pressed both sheets to her chest and looked up, first at Doc Coates, then at Holt, and cleared her throat.

"Both forms confirm a familial match. Holt's DNA is a fifty percent match to yours, Doc," she said, favoring him with a smile. "The rest," she said, turning back to Holt, "must be your mother's. You've found your father, Holt! Merry Christmas." She stepped forward and hugged him.

Knees suddenly weak, Holt wanted to hang on, grateful for Caitlin's support. But she pulled away, turned and gave his father a hug. His father. The words sounded strangely alien in his mind.

When Caitlin stepped back, she shifted her gaze to Holt and tilted her head. Her message couldn't be any more clear.

He did as she suggested and stepped toward his father,

hand extended, but the vet pulled him into a hug. Chauncey gave a warning yip, but they ignored him.

"I can't believe this is real," Coates said. "But I'm glad it is." He pounded on Holt's back for a moment, then let him go.

Holt cleared his throat, wishing there was some way he could wipe the dampness from his eyes without looking like a total wuss. "I never expected to have a father in my life. I'm glad he turned out to be you. I'm really proud of what you did here tonight." He reached down and patted Chauncey's head. "What you do every day. I was going to tell you, no matter how those turned out," Holt said and tipped his head toward the lab reports Caitlin still held, "that I want to help."

Coates met his gaze. "Thank you. I don't know what to say, except that I'm glad, too. More than I ever imagined I could be. Look what you've made of yourself, despite the rough start you had thanks to Jenny's aunt. I couldn't be more proud if I'd raised you myself." Then he turned to Caitlin. "And you, my Scottish friend, I wonder if all this would have happened if you hadn't been mugged your first day in the village…"

"And ye hadna come to my rescue," Caitlin answered, her thicker accent and the gravel in her voice revealing how choked up she was by the revelations. "We wouldna kenned what could ha' been, and that would ha' been a tragedy." A tear tracked down her cheek, then another, and another, where they met the corners of her smile.

"But it wasn't," Holt interjected, feeling giddy bubbles fizzing through his bloodstream. Was this happiness? If so, he had missed a lot in his life. "You weren't hurt that day, and you made a friend who turned out to be important in my life. Both our lives. Even more, you stuck by your guns when I didn't believe in you or your wild theories. You were right all along. I'm glad you didn't let me push you around."

"I'm a Scot. We don't push very easily," Caitlin told him, her smile turning into a grin.

His father laughed at that. "Holt, I think you've met your match."

Caitlin's eyes widened, and her mouth dropped open, but a warm sense of rightness filled Holt with those words. His father was right. He had met his match. He'd known for days and had begun the conversation about their future together before the outcry by the Christmas tree broke the spell. He had more to do to convince Caitlin, but he never doubted for a moment that he would succeed.

~

Christmas day arrived with unfinished business between Holt and Caitlin. He entered his great-aunt's closet with more than a little trepidation, but he was on a mission, one he'd nearly left until too late. In her jewelry box, he hoped to find a ring he could give Caitlin. Something important enough to show her how much she meant to him, but not so gaudy that she might not like it. If nothing else, a placeholder until she could select a ring herself. *If she said yes.*

The box's small brass lock plate was locked, but he had

the keyring he'd found hidden in a drawer, the same one that held the key they'd used to unlock the trunk in the attic— and a host of family secrets. This lock opened easily, proof that his great-aunt had used it often. He lifted the lid.

Ornate gemstone earrings and a string of pearls filled the top drawer. The next drawer held marcasite jewelry, very old-fashioned. No. Nothing interested him until he opened the third drawer. Pay dirt! Rings filled it. The diamonds needed to be cleaned. He couldn't judge their quality, but their cut was also old-fashioned. A sapphire encrusted band caught his eye, but right under it, he found a small yellow silk drawstring bag. He opened it carefully and spilled the contents into his palm. A large, clear, deep green, emerald-cut emerald set in yellow gold winked green and gold at him. He studied it, looking for flaws and found none. Perfect. He dropped it back into its protective bag and locked the box, but he wondered that she kept valuable jewelry in the house like this and not in a safe. The house was isolated, but that didn't guarantee anything.

Now to finish his preparations. He gave the ring to Mrs. Smith, then he went in search of Caitlin.

Weeks ago, when he found out about his inheritance, all he'd felt was dread. He had never dreamed he could be as happy as Caitlin made him. Knowing she cared about him — not his wealth— meant everything. She had done her best to make his life better— often despite him.

He found her in the office, puttering with the catalog of his great-aunt's belongings. "I thought you'd finished that," he told her. "It's Christmas, not a day to work."

She pointed at the screen and shrugged. "I can never

leave well enough alone. I thought of a more appealing way to describe some of the furniture, so here I am. What are you up to?"

He glanced out the window in time to see Mrs. Smith walking back toward the house. Holt gave Caitlin his best innocent, *I'm not up to anything* look. "Grab your coat and come with me?"

"Sure. Where?"

"You'll see."

Caitlin closed her laptop and left the room, giving him a quizzical glance as she passed him by and stepped out of the office door. He'd left his jacket in the foyer in case he talked her into going out with him. By the time he donned his, she was back, buttoning up her coat as she approached. "Okay, I've wearing my coat. Now, where are we going?"

"Come with me." Earlier, Holt had realized the perfect place to pop the question. He led Caitlin to the old gazebo, where Mrs. Smith had set up a table draped with a white cloth and covered with a tea service, a thermos, small cakes, and other sweets. Holt didn't expect they'd enjoy any of it but figured it was good camouflage.

"It's still a bit chilly out here for tea, don't you think?"

"Really? A hardy Scot concerned about the cold?" He gave her a disarming grin. When she rolled her eyes, he added, "I thought some hot tea would be just the thing to warm our first Christmas together while we enjoyed the day."

"Um, okay." Caitlin set about pouring tea. "You take yours black, aye?"

"And you take yours with milk and an ungodly amount

of sugar, yes," Holt replied with a grin. "Don't forget a sweet or two."

"Ha! Ye ken my weakness," Caitlin answered, chuckling. Then she froze, tongs held a few inches above the serving plate. "Wait. What's this?" She looked up at Holt, brow furrowed.

He knew exactly what she'd found in the middle of the tea cakes. He dropped to one knee and held out a hand. "That, my love, is a ring. A complete circle, a symbol of my infinitely deep feelings for you. And the emerald symbolizes new beginnings, growth, and love. Forever love. I want you in my life forever, Caitlin. Will you marry me?"

She picked up the ring and held it out to him.

Holt's heart plummeted, fearing that she was about to refuse him.

"I've never seen an emerald this big, Holt. I'm no' used to your world. Your wealth." She paused and swallowed. "Are ye sure I'm the lass for ye?"

"As sure as I've ever been of anything, Caitlin. Say yes. Please say yes. If you don't like that ring, you can pick out another one you do like. Or one for each finger."

She made him wait. He wasn't surprised, just fearful. His chest felt too tight for his heart to have room to beat, his muscles locked so hard, holding him in place on one knee, that he thought he might start to shake. She wasn't going to make anything easy for him, but he loved that about her. She was her own woman, used to making her own decisions. While she thought, she glanced from him to the ring to him several times, and Holt held his breath.

"'Tis a beauty, and I love it. But I love ye more, Holt Ridley. Yes! Aye, I'll marry ye."

He rose to meet her as she fell into his arms. "I've never been so happy," he whispered to her. "I don't know how."

"But you'll enjoy learning," Caitlin told him. "I'll teach you. I promise you that."

~

Christmas night arrived, and Caitlin had to wrap tape around the shank of the emerald ring to make it fit her finger. Holt promised they'd get it sized in town the next day. In the meantime, she refused to go without it.

Tonight, they would host their first Christmas dinner celebration. The first of many, she hoped, though not for any concern about the Ridley family curse. The apothecary chest was safely stored at Cairn Dubh in the Highlands where it belonged. Instead, she hoped for years of happiness with Holt, his father and their friends as well as with her family in Scotland. She looked forward to many celebrations, large and small, public and intimate, and most especially, with the children she hoped they would make together, the family Holt never believed he would have.

While Holt conferred with Farrell, she looked around her, struggling to take in the changes a few event-filled weeks had wrought. The house was decorated beautifully. Mrs. Smith had worked her magic in the kitchen, and Caitlin and Holt had worked all day with Farrell to expand the festive holiday mood in the house that they'd first created with the Christmas trees. Now wreaths and roping adorned with lights and colorful balls draped doorways and mantels. Smaller ornaments and other seasonal decorations enhanced occasional tables beside chairs and in front of couches. The dinner table was set for a feast and decorated with candles, greenery and more colorful glass balls. Their guests would arrive soon. She couldn't wait.

Holt's father arrived first. Holt took him aside after Caitlin greeted him and left them to their reunion. Tears filled her eyes to see them with their heads together, deep in conversation. They finally had the family neither thought to ever have. She didn't know what Holt wanted to discuss with him, but both had a glint of tears in their eyes, though being manly, they refused to shed them. Whatever it was, it clearly meant something important to both of them. She was thrilled to have helped bring Holt a happy resolution to the misery of his childhood and the sorry history of his family.

Their friends began to arrive soon after. Alice looked wonderful in her Christmas finery. This was the first time Caitlin could recall having seen her out of her white baker's jacket and her red dress fit her like a dream. She caught Holt's father studying Alice as Holt introduced them and fought a grin. Apparently, he liked the way she looked, as well. Rachel was there, too. She had mentioned to Caitlin that Doc Coates had sent her to Alice's bakery several times for more chocolate croissants, but from the way his gaze followed Alice now, she would bet he hadn't yet gone there himself and was regretting it. Caitlin suspected after tonight, he would become a regular customer. And perhaps more.

The next to arrive were high school friends of Holt's, Jack and Anita from Holt's favorite pizza parlor. That declaration earned Holt a laugh. The lawyer and estate's executor, Mr. Thornton, evened out the number for the dinner table. Caitlin was especially pleased to see him. His presence was a measure of how Holt's attitude had changed about the estate and everything in it.

"Now that everyone is here," Holt said as Farrell passed out glasses of champagne, then returned to the kitchen. "I'd like to make a Christmas toast." He raised his glass. "To family," he said with a nod to his newfound father. "To friends," he added with a smile for everyone else, "and to a wonderful Christmas for us all. I don't know how to express how much it means to me to have you all here."

Caitlin didn't know if it was apparent to anyone else, but she'd heard the catch in Holt's voice before he lifted his glass.

"Hear! Hear!" Jack said as everyone raised their glass in response, then drank.

Perhaps his friend Jack knew him well enough to have noticed it. Caitlin gave him a smile of thanks for diverting attention for the moment Holt needed to collect himself.

"Dinner is served," Farrell eventually announced in his best butler imitation.

Everyone filed into the dining room and took their seats. Caitlin had made place cards and seated Alice across from Holt's father to make conversation— or longing looks— easier for them. If they got to know each other, there might be another Christmas miracle.

Holt waited until everyone got settled, then addressed the table. "I have a few announcements to make before we eat." He held out a hand for Caitlin.

She took his and rose, embarrassed, yet excited, knowing what he planned to say next.

"The first, in case you haven't noticed," he said, holding up her hand and turning it so the ring was visible to all, "is that Caitlin Paterson has agreed to become my wife."

Whoops, cheers, and clapping greeted that announcement. Caitlin felt herself blush, heat rising from her chest to her cheeks as Holt pulled her to him and kissed her.

When their guests quieted down, and she had a chance to catch her breath, he added, "I've also made a decision about this estate that affects you all, and one I hope you will approve."

Caitlin froze. He hadn't told her about this. Why not? Had he found a local buyer? Nay, she didn't think that was it. If he hoped they'd approve, he must not plan to sell it.

Holt's steady gaze soothed Caitlin's fears. He would have warned her if he knew she'd be upset. She took a breath and nodded.

He looked around the table. "I'm not going to sell the estate." He paused to let everyone breathe a sigh of relief, then a smile lit his face. "I'm going to turn it over to Doc Coates to create the canine rescue and training facility that is my father's dream. Mrs. Smith and Farrell will stay on, of course, to help my father manage the estate."

Caitlin noticed Mr. Thornton nod and realized Holt

had cleared this with him ahead of time, as executor of the estate and person in charge of dealing with the mountain of paperwork such an endeavor would likely require. She had every confidence Thornton could handle it.

"What do you mean, your father?" Alice asked, looking at Coates, who gave her a quirk of his lips.

"That's my third happy announcement. Due almost entirely to Caitlin's dogged persistence, and nothing could be more appropriate than that term," he added and favored her with a grin, "Jim Coates and I have discovered— and proven via DNA tests— that he is the father I never knew. And I am the son he never knew he had." He raised a hand to silence the gasps and clapping that greeted his announcement. "It's a long story that we'll share after dinner. After all her hard work, I don't want to keep Mrs. Smith's wonderful meal waiting."

Mrs. Smith and Farrell brought out the soup course, then salad, and so on, until no one could eat another bite. Holt stood and called for the chef. When she appeared, he announced. "Thank you, Mrs. Smith. You've outdone yourself. Farrell, too," Holt added with a nod to the man standing behind Mrs. Smith. "Without both of you, this estate would have fallen to ruin years ago. I'm glad you both are staying on. I trust you will enjoy working with my father and his team for many years."

The lady in question dimpled and quit the room to applause, Farrell, with a pleased nod, followed her out.

"Let's adjourn to the front room for dessert and drinks," Holt invited.

Caitlin was pleased to see Holt's father move quickly to

take Alice's arm and escort her from the table. Her plan seemed to be working. In the front room, she took Holt aside for a moment. "I love what you're doing with the estate. Doc Coates will make good use of it. And how wonderful that Farrell and Mrs. Smith will be able to stay on and take care of it. I'm so glad everything has worked out so well."

"Everything has worked out perfectly," he told her. "Especially you." He lifted her hand and ran his thumb over the emerald ring. "I just hope you're not planning on a long engagement," he told her with a wicked grin.

"Nay, I'm not. But let's talk about that later. Our guests are watching us."

Holt kissed her. "Let them watch," he said, then wrapped her in his arms and kissed her again.

Caitlin ignored the laughter and clapping, lost in the feel of Holt's lips on hers. When he broke the kiss, she pulled him down for another, then stepped out of his arms and turned to their guests. And family. "We're so happy you're here. Holt will pour whatever you'd like, then we'll tell all."

Doc Coates was grinning, but not at her. His gaze was on Alice, who shared a small settee with him. Alice was laughing, then her expression sobered to a quizzical smile as he picked up her hand.

Caitlin glanced at Holt to see if he noticed. His smile told her he had. Well, then, two Christmas miracles, coming right up. With dessert, she thought, as Mrs. Smith wheeled in a cart loaded with bite-sized sweets and slim bottles of dessert wines. Could this evening get any better?

Later, after Caitlin overheard Doc Coates and Alice making a date for the next evening, their guests— and family— departed. Holt took Caitlin in his arms. "What a Christmas for miracles. I feel like the three magi dropped by and each left a wonderful surprise, you being the best of all."

"Not finding your father?"

"As pleased as I am about that, to borrow another reference from literature, he is…well, not the ghost of my past, but he is my past. Tonight is our present, and you, my lovely Caitlin, are my future."

EPILOGUE

"Ah, Scotland," Caitlin exulted, taking a deep breath as they exited the terminal. Holt's pilot had brought them to Glasgow in time for an early morning landing. The sun peeked through broken clouds, and the air was crisp if slightly tinged with the scent of jet fuel.

"Glad to be back?" Holt nodded to a driver holding a sign with his name on it and handed over their luggage.

After he helped Caitlin into the waiting limo, she smiled. "I am. But happiest to be here with ye. I canna wait to show ye around."

"I'm sorry we didn't make it for Hogmanay. You were looking forward to it."

Caitlin shrugged, knowing how important the time in New York had been to him. "You had too much to do before you could leave, and I didn't want to go without you. We'll plan to be here next year." She grinned and added, "I had enough excitement over the holiday in New York to satisfy me."

She pointed out some sights as they drove away from the airport's vicinity, then pulled out her phone. "I almost forgot to text Ian we're on the way."

Holt put a hand on her forearm. "Wait. Before you do that, I have a question. I know you planned for this trip to go a certain way…"

Caitlin's stomach clenched. Was Holt getting cold feet? Why now and not before they flew to Scotland? "What do you mean?"

"Visiting your cousin, touring around." He held up a hand. "I want to do all of that, but first, I have something else in mind." He took her hands in his larger ones. "Let's not wait. I want to marry you— right away. As soon as we can arrange it. Then we'll travel as you planned, and we'll enjoy the journey even more."

"Do ye mean it? I thought ye'd want to meet my family first, to see where I come from."

"You know I do. But none of that will change how I feel about you. And you did say you wanted a short engagement." His gaze turned molten. "Let's make the arrangements as soon as we can."

Elation made Caitlin's blood sizzle. "Let's. Nothing would make me happier."

Holt lifted her hands and kissed the back of each before they settled into the limo's plush upholstery to enjoy the scenery. As they drove deeper into the Highlands and familiar landmarks appeared, Caitlin's excitement mounted. Once they turned into the long drive leading to Cairn Dubh, she told Holt, "We're here."

Ian, Lara, and the twins greeted them at the door. Lara hugged her, saying, "I was just headed out to take the twins to school, but I'll be back before you know it. I made coffee," she added with a smile for Holt. "But if you'd rather have tea, Caitlin knows where everything is."

Caitlin gave Lara and the twins another hug and let them go on their way. A few minutes later, she and Holt found themselves settled in the kitchen with Ian and coffee.

"The furnishings from Holt's estate have been here for over a month," she said after a restorative sip. "Have you noticed anything…different?" Along with the cursed cabinet, they'd shipped other pieces Caitlin thought might have come from the same household, owing to their similar construction and condition. Ian had taken charge of them until Caitlin could arrive to make appropriate arrangements for them.

"Nothing to report," Ian told her. "We've noticed nothing unusual since they arrived."

"Nothing more unusual than the usual for Cairn Dubh, ye mean." Caitlin felt tension ease out of her that she hadn't realized she carried.

"Aye. Fergus seems unconcerned. The twins would have said something. They're more attuned to him than the grown-ups."

"That's good, aye, that Fergus is calm about it all?" Of course, it was.

"As near as I can tell, aye, it is." Ian shrugged, then regarded Holt steadily.

Holt nodded.

"So ye ken about our wee beastie."

"Caitlin has told me a little about your protective ghost."

That seemed to be what Ian wanted to hear. "You've got an itinerary worked out, then?" he asked, clearly ready to change the subject.

Caitlin nodded, then glanced at Holt to make sure he didn't object. "We'd planned on a few days here to get settled and get over jet lag. Holt has never been to Scotland, so I've much to show him. We'll make our way to Inverness from there where I hope to work out a deal with the Highland Museum to display the pieces and do a story about the curse. I still hope to consult there, if not to become a permanent member of the staff." She hesitated, then plunged ahead. "Then on to Edinburgh. We'd planned to return here in about a fortnight for the wedding, but Holt…"

"Has other ideas," Holt interrupted, taking her hand. "I want us to marry as soon as possible."

Ian grinned. "An eager bridegroom. Aye, well, then, ye'll need Lara to help ye with that. She should be back soon after half nine."

"I was going to wait until tonight to spring this on ye," Caitlin agreed, "but I'll tell her when she gets back. She and I can work out what needs to be done over tea and scones."

"Brilliant. I'll take Holt into the village with me." He gave Holt a grin. "Trust me, when those two lasses put their heads together, 'tis best to be as far from them as ye can be.

Leave them to their lists. They'll have plenty for us to do, all too soon."

Holt winked at Caitlin and laughed. "I'll take you up on that, Ian. I've seen Caitlin at work." At Caitlin's frown, he added, "She's a whirlwind of the very best kind."

"Decided to save yerself, did ye?" Caitlin narrowed her eyes, teasing. "We willna want the two of ye underfoot, as Ian kens fine." She stood. "Why don't we get settled while I wait for Lara, then ye two can escape."

Holt got to his feet and took her hand. "Lay on, MacDuff..."

Caitlin rolled her eyes, gave grinning Ian a wave, and led Holt back to the foyer to pick up their bags, then upstairs to his room. "I'm across the hall," she told him. "There are two very intelligent, very inquisitive twins in the house who notice everything. I think we should keep our sleeping arrangements this way until the wedding."

"They're not here now."

"Nay, but Ian is. And Lara will be home soon. Get cleaned up. I'm going to unpack while I have the chance." She tugged her bag from Holt's hand, pulling him toward her in the process.

Holt leaned in to give her a kiss, then went obediently into his room.

~

Hours later, Holt returned from the village with Ian. As he climbed the stairs in search of Caitlin, he could hear Lara telling her husband that she and Caitlin had worked up lists of what had to be done and by whom. Ian's low rumble became unintelligible as Holt turned a corner in the upstairs hall, and Caitlin's voice came to him from her room.

"That's perfect. I'm so happy you can arrange it."

Holt entered the room as she glanced around with her phone to her ear, saw him and colored.

"I'll speak to you later. Thank you," she added and ended the call.

"Who was that? I heard Lara tell Ian that you two have everything organized."

"Organized, aye. And lots still to be done." She gestured with the phone. "I'll be on this for hours until the day." She glanced at it, then lifted her gaze back to him and smiled.

Holt couldn't escape the sense that she was hiding something. Her Scottish accent had thickened since she'd returned home, but now, on the phone, she sounded more like she had by the time they left Long Island.

"So, how was your trip to town with Ian?" She tossed her phone on the bed and came into his arms. "What did you do?"

Holt held her for a moment, just soaking in the feeling of Caitlin in his arms, her scent surrounding him, her warmth heating his blood. Then he dipped his head and kissed her.

"Ah, visited the pub, did ye?"

"We had a dram. Medicinal purposes. Ian claimed whiskey is a great cure for jet lag."

She snorted. "Ian's blowing sunshine up yer skirt."

Holt laughed, picturing himself in a kilt, then sobered,

realizing Caitlin and her cousins might expect him to wear one to the wedding. That would be among many new experiences he suspected Caitlin had planned for him.

Caitlin leaned back in his arms, her brows drawn together. "Isn't that your American saying?"

He kissed the crease and nodded. "You got it exactly right."

Lara's voice intruded as she called up the stairs. "Anyone hungry? I've got lunch."

"On our way," Caitlin replied, calling over Holt's shoulder.

"Not just yet," he murmured and kissed her again, this time on the mouth. "I can never get enough of this. Of you."

With a grin, she reached down and poked him in the belly. "You need food on top of that whiskey. Kisses won't absorb it."

"Who said I want them to?" He laughed and released her, then took her hand. "Shall we?"

Caitlin stepped close and kissed him back, surprising him, and then led him downstairs.

~

Three mornings later, Caitlin and Holt went to the registrar for the marriage license. Afterwards, Holt met Ian for help finding the clothes and other things he needed for what Ian deemed would be a proper Scottish ceremony and *ceilidh* to follow it.

Lara and Caitlin went by Caitlin's flat to gather what

she needed from there. She didn't know whether she'd sell the flat or keep it for a home base between trips. She and Holt hadn't had a chance to discuss what their living arrangements might be after they completed the tour of Scotland Caitlin wanted to take him on. But that decision would wait. Even if they gave up her flat, they wouldn't be homeless. Cairn Dubh boasted so many suites, they could live there indefinitely and never be in the way of the family.

After she and Lara finished at the flat, they went to the High street to shop for a dress, flowers, and accessories before picking up the twins from school. Once they were in the car, Amy leaned forward in her seatbelt and rested her elbows on the back of Caitlin's seat. "Did you get everything?"

Caitlin glanced around and nodded. "We did! It's all in the boot."

"I can't wait to see your dress," Amy declared. "Will you show me as soon as we get home?"

Alex stared out the side window, expressing supreme masculine disinterest in all things wedding-related. Amy opened her mouth to ask another question, but after a glance in her rear-view mirror, Lara interrupted, "Sit back, young lady. You'll see everything in good time."

Amy settled back, but Caitlin could see she was still bristling with questions.

"I don't suppose anyone in this car would like to be my flower girl?"

"Aye!" Amy pumped her arm in triumph. "I will." She poked her brother's ribs. "I'm going to be in the wedding!"

"And Alex, would you like to be in charge of the rings?"

"Isn't that what *weans* do? I'm too old."

"Not always, and it's a very important job," Caitlin told him. "The rings are valuable, ye ken. And ye'd be helping your soon-to-be uncle Holt and your da." Cousin, actually, but she could never keep all the first-, second-, and distant-cousin definitions straight, much less the spouses of cousins. Uncle was easier. Besides, they already called her *Auntie Caitlin,* ever since their mother married her cousin Ian. Caitlin took care of the twins during their mother's honeymoon absence.

Alex poked his sister back, then met Caitlin's gaze with his serious one and nodded. "I guess I could do that, aye."

She very carefully didn't look at Lara. Alex would see a grin, even a side-eye glance between them in the rear-view mirror and might change his mind. "Then it's settled. Everyone has a part to play in the wedding."

An hour after they got home, a knock sounded at Cairn Dubh's front door. Lara looked up to Holt from the early dinner she and Caitlin were making. "Can you get that, please? The twins are doing homework. Ian, can you help me here for a moment?"

Holt nodded and left the kitchen where he and Ian had been sitting, watching the women, and offering commentary.

As soon as he left the room, Caitlin and Lara grabbed towels to wipe their hands and gathered up Ian with a look. They arrived in the front foyer just as Holt opened the door, then stiffened.

"I heard there's a bachelor pub crawl tonight. I didn't

want to miss it." Doc Coates and Alice Nash stood on the front porch. A limo driver set their luggage behind them, doffed his cap and left.

Holt grinned and pulled his father into a hug. "I can't believe you're here. You said you couldn't get away from your practice. Or your bakery," he added as he hugged Alice.

"We lied. We couldn't miss this!" Alice reached for Holt's hand. "I'm thrilled to be here."

Holt's father put an arm around Alice's shoulders. "We both are."

Caitlin watched their reunion with tears stinging her eyes, then caught Holt's gaze. "Surprise!"

Holt stepped back to let the older couple enter the house, then gathered her up in his arms. "It's the best surprise," he whispered in Caitlin's ear. "Thank you."

The next day, Holt surprised her by coming downstairs wearing the full Scottish ceremonial outfit of kilt in a Black Watch plaid, short jacket and all the accessories. Ian was dressed similarly in one of the family tartans. Caitlin and Lara eyed their men, then glanced at each other and smiled. Ian had worked a miracle convincing Holt to wear a kilt, and the deep Black Watch colors of the rented outfit suited him. He might have chosen something different if there'd been time to have something made, but Caitlin approved. He wore it very well and looked even more handsome than she'd imagined he might in something that, if he wore it the traditional way, must make him uncomfortable. It wasn't easy, but she pulled her imagination away from the image that thought evoked. Instead, she glanced down at herself. Her simple tea-length dress of cream silk with pearl buttons down the front would stand out beautifully in pictures against his deeper colors.

"You two make a gorgeous couple," Lara exclaimed.

Caitlin could feel the warmth of a blush heating her face as Holt's gaze raked over her, approval and desire in his eyes.

"Then let's not waste it," Holt said. "Let's get married."

Caitlin laughed and took the arm he proffered. "Aye. Let's!"

The whole family went to the registrar for the official ceremony tying the knot. Caitlin waited on the side wall at the back of the room where she could see everyone. Amy carried a basket toward the front, handing flowers to people sitting along both sides of the center aisle, many their guests, and some waiting for other ceremonies. Normally effusive, she fulfilled her role as flower girl with more solemnity than Caitlin thought she would be able to manage. The flower recipients reacted with smiles and murmured thanks, clearly pleased with Amy's gift. When she reached the front, she stood in line with her mother and Alice. Alex went next with the wedding rings on a deep rose-pink, silk pillow, looking proud, but also slightly embarrassed every time he noticed a lass near his age watching him. When he reached the front, he stood with his father and Holt, clutching the small pillow with its simple gold bands on top in both hands.

Caitlin met Holt's smoldering gaze. How would she make it up the aisle at a sedate walk when all she wanted to do was run into his arms? But she had to wait.

Caitlin hadn't told Holt she had asked Doc Coates to do the honors and give her away. It surprised her that he hadn't realized his father was missing, since Alice stood beside Lara opposite Holt and Ian, but perhaps Holt thought he was on a quick trip to the men's room. He was, though not for the usual reason. She loved Holt's reaction when his father entered the room also dressed in a Black Watch plaid kilt Ian had arranged and took up his position beside her.

Holt's jaw dropped, and his gaze kept shifting between her and his father. His color was high, and the glow in his eyes shone with love.

She took his father's arm. He lifted her hand and kissed the back, then gave her a proud smile. They made their way slowly up the aisle to where Holt and Ian stood in front of the registrar.

A glimmer of tears also sheened Jim Coates' eyes when he kissed her cheek and gave her hand into his son's keeping. Holt gave his father a one-armed hug, then pulled Caitlin to his side. Still holding her hand, he leaned his mouth next to her ear and whispered, "Perfection."

The civil ceremony was short, as Caitlin expected, since she'd watched the same registrar marry Ian and Lara nearly a year ago. But the ceremony was new to Holt. She kept her gaze on him rather than the registrar. Holt's locked on her, as well, as he repeated the required legal declarations, then listened to hers. Alex gave the rings to his father, and Ian provided hers to Holt and Holt's to her for the exchange.

As Holt slipped the gold ring on her finger, he

murmured, "Ye are mine, and I am yours." He vowed, softly but with fervor, "Forever."

"Forever," she repeated the only vow that mattered, slid his ring on his hand. With the possible exception of Holt's father, if anyone else heard their declaration, they would not understand the significance of that one word. But to Holt, and to her, with his family history, it meant everything.

Once the registrar declared them wed, Holt wasted no time pulling her against him for a searing kiss that raised a cheer from everyone watching, many of whom were waving the flowers Amy had provided. Caitlin kissed him back, blushed, and smiled at their audience as her new father-in-law, Lara, and Alice began taking pictures.

After signing the required marriage schedule and taking a few more pictures inside the ceremony room, they moved outside to a nearby park to take more photos among the trees and flowers, and to give their guests time to reach Cairn Dubh before them.

Finally, Caitlin called a halt, and they headed for the reception. Lara preceded her to the new wing and made her pause out of sight of the great hall's double-door opening, but Caitlin sneaked peeks around the edge of the doors into the large chamber. It was a beautiful space, filled with sunshine on this early spring afternoon. Rainbows glinted on the white walls from the sun shining through the crystal chandeliers, and the gilt edging glowed on the moldings at the top of the walls and the painted copies of medieval illuminations of fanciful beasts and flowers that covered the ceiling.

The reception area boasted an open bar and a dance floor for the *ceilidh* to follow the meal. Tables decorated with ribbons and flowers filled the rest of the expansive space. A harpist played, the music as bright and delightful as their surroundings. Servers stood ready to deliver the catered dinner from the secondary kitchen and butler's pantry off of the great hall, and a photographer stood by to take candid shots of the rest of the evening.

Caitlin smiled as Amy took her seat at the head table. The flower girl had been a highlight of the ceremony. Alex joined her, relief to be done with his part in the wedding evident in his suddenly relaxed posture as he slumped into his seat, pulled the silk pillow from his sporran and tossed it to his sister. Lara frowned at Alex, and he straightened up in his seat, then she turned to Caitlin and shrugged.

Caitlin grinned as Holt and Ian joined them. It was time to get the party started. Lara and Ian made their entrance first, a signal that the bride and groom had truly arrived. Caitlin expected to follow close behind them, but Holt held her back, letting his father and Alice precede them. Once all four had reached the long head table, Holt held up her hand. "Ready?"

"Aye, for hours," Caitlin told him and pulled him forward with a laugh. That drew attention to them, so they savored their walk up the center aisle as they paused to greet guests who reached out to them along the way.

During the reception, Holt met Caitlin's friends and withstood friendly ribbing about not being able to find a suitable American girl.

"Only a Highland lass would do," he boasted, with a smile for his new bride.

"I've married a wise man," Caitlin responded. "But I already knew that."

After having a few dances and making the rounds of their guests, once they had a moment to themselves, Holt told her, "I have a present for you, my lovely wife." The other guests were drinking gallons of champagne, whiskey, and gin, talking and laughing so loudly that, combined with the dance music, they created a bubble of privacy around the newlyweds.

Caitlin displayed the emerald on her left hand and smiled. "Ye gave me a beauty already, my handsome husband."

"Ah, but there's more. I got a call this morning from my lawyers. I've sold my company in California. We're free to live here or Inverness near the museum or anywhere you like."

"Holt! Why didn't you tell me?" She wasn't sure her heart could stand any more happiness today, but elation filled her again at Holt's news.

"I just did. It's what I spent so much time working on the last week we were at the estate and since then. A friend bought into it. He'll manage the company well. I still have a block of shares, but I've given up my controlling interest. I'm starting fresh with you. Aren't you happy?"

"I'm thrilled. I'm just surprised. Gobsmacked. You built that company from nothing."

"And sold it for a handsome profit."

"What will you do?"

"Besides spend hours making love to my gorgeous wife? Anything I want. Eventually, I'll start another company. But not right away. I plan to enjoy a lengthy honeymoon. If that's all right with you."

Caitlin stroked his cheek. "It sounds perfect." Holt had just given her everything she could have hoped for— and more. In New York, she'd learned that time with him, unfettered by concerns about his business, was precious. Her heart felt full to bursting. She didn't know whether to laugh or let everyone in the room see her tears of joy.

"Then we'll live here, at least for now," Holt told her as he wiped a tear from her cheek with his thumb. "We'll raise Ridley heirs," he added with a smile, "of which there will be many, now that you solved the family curse. We'll find a place you like, a home base to return to between trips. There's so much of the world I want to show you."

"And so much more of Scotland I want to show you. But all that will wait. 'Tis our wedding night. I believe we already have plans."

"Shall we bid goodnight to everyone or just slip away?"

Caitlin glanced around, suddenly eager to leave the party. "The latter, I think. They're so far in their cups, they won't notice we've gone until morning. Just be patient."

"About being alone with you? Not a chance."

Holt stood and took her hand, pulling her up beside him. Caitlin clung to him, not quite willing to accept that all this was true. She was married to Holt Ridley. The massive emerald on her hand tied her to him as surely as the papers they'd signed earlier that day. They would be able to live in Scotland for as long as she wished. He'd even implied he had no problem with her working at the Highland Museum and living near it. He'd given up his company for her. What more could she ask, except that he love her for all of their very long lives together?

A movement made Caitlin glance over Holt's shoulder in time to see Fergus appear in the doorway that led to the hallway and to the stairs to their bridal chamber. She gave the ghost hound a smile, and instead of simply disappearing, he turned and walked back into the hall behind him. Even Fergus thought it was time for them to leave the party. She was more than ready, and from the smile lighting Holt's face and the molten look turning his grey eyes black, he was, too.

"I hope you know where we're going," he told her as they moved toward the door where Fergus had disappeared. Their friends let them go with smiles and cheers, a few slapping Holt on the back as they went, or taking Caitlin's hand for a moment to voice their well-wishes.

Once clear of the hall, Holt said, "I still get lost in this wing, much less in the entire house. And when is that ghost going to show himself? I thought you said he liked weddings."

"I know exactly where I'm taking you, husband. And Fergus was here just moments ago, agreeing with us that it was time to quit the party."

"Smart dog."

"Aye, he is. Now that we've time, I'll tell you more about him."

"Later," Holt advised as they mounted the stairs to the top floor and the suite of chambers set aside for them.

Fergus awaited them at the door to their bower. "Aye, later." She gave the ghost a stern look, hoping he'd take the hint. "We're going to be busy—"

Fergus stepped aside, but didn't disappear.

"For hours. Days," Holt said, pulled her into his arms and kissed her, his lips moving over hers softly at first, then firmly, teasing her, making her blood heat with wanting him.

"Nights," Caitlin breathed between kisses. She was tempted to tell Holt that Fergus was standing right next to him, studying him as if deciding whether or not he approved, but she decided the friendly ghost might be a distraction for Holt that she didn't want right now. She reached aside and opened the door, then shrieked with laughter when Holt suddenly picked her up.

Taking the hint, Fergus made himself scarce.

"I must carry you across the threshold," Holt reminded her. "I don't want to fail in the first of my husbandly duties."

"You're doing a brilliant job of it so far," Caitlin told him, giddy with excitement, and relieved that Fergus understood to leave them alone.

"I've had a lot of practice carrying you. I like it."

She curled her fingers into his hair, tugging gently. "I wonder if you'll like the rest of your husbandly duties as well."

He pushed the door closed with his shoulder and set her on her feet, his gaze molten with promise. "Once I lock this, I'll be happy to show you. Forever."

THE END

Don't miss Book One, Ian Paterson and Lara MacLaren's romance and mystery (and Fergus!) in *WAITING FOR THE LAIRD*.

And coming in 2025, look for Book Three, Doc Coates' and Alice Nash's later-in-life love story.

ALSO BY WILLA BLAIR

Highland Talents Heritage

Highland Prodigy

Highland Memories

Highland Reckoning

Highland Dreamer

Highland Echo

His Highland Heart

His Highland Rose

His Highland Heart

His Highland Love

His Highland Bride

Laird of Lies

His Highland Heart Boxed Set

Highland Talents

Heart of Stone

Highland Healer

Highland Seer

Highland Troth

The Healer's Gift

When Highland Lightning Strikes

Love Lost

Waiting for the Laird

Waiting for a Forever Love

Other Novels

When You Find Love

Highland Beginnings

ABOUT THE AUTHOR

Willa Blair is an award-wining Amazon and Barnes & Noble #1 bestselling author of Scottish historical, light paranormal and contemporary romance, filled with men in kilts, psi talents, and plenty of spice. Her books have won numerous accolades, including the Marlene, the Merritt, National Readers' Choice Award Finalist, Booksellers' Best Award Finalist, National Excellence in Story Telling Historical Fiction Third Place Winner, Reader's Crown finalist, InD'Tale Magazine's RONE Award Honorable Mention, and NightOwl Reviews Top Picks. She loves scouting new settings for books, and thinks being an author is the best job she's ever had.

Willa loves hearing from readers!
Contact her:
www.willablair.com
authorwillablair@gmail.com

Sign up for my Newsletter
Find links to the rest of my books

Milton Keynes UK
Ingram Content Group UK Ltd.
UKHW040358111224
452348UK00004B/278

9 781648 397714